The Alien's Treat
Alien Snack Searcher Book 1
Alina Riley

Chapter 1

Serena

I let out a soft sigh after all the dough is in the oven, rising and getting ready. I check again to make sure the timer is running with the right settings.

This is the perfect time of the day for me. I'm mostly alone in the kitchen and I get to prepare doughnuts for the shop. Soon, there will be customers, and I hope they will be happy with what I prepared for them.

There's a ding from the storefront, so I go out front to help the customer. Early mornings are always tough when it comes to service. It's up to me until later in the day and I have someone in to help.

I smile at the hulky, coal-gray male at the counter. "Good morning, how can I help?" He is standing there, with his hands in his pocket.

He gives me a nod and peeks at the kitchen where I came out from. "Doughnuts?"

I glance at where he is looking before turning back to him. "They won't be ready for another half an hour." Maybe he is a new customer, who I always welcome.

He frowns and checks his phone. Maybe he's in a hurry. I shrug. "Sorry about that, but we aim to serve fresh doughnuts daily, so it takes time to get them ready." I pull out a leaflet and hand it to him. "Here you go. It has the time when the doughnuts are ready. You can wait on your spaceship if you want to."

He checks out the leaflet and groans. "So you open the shop without anything to sell?"

"I can grab you a coffee if you want. You can take a seat over there, by the windows."

He looks over there. There are tables and chairs with potted plants. Most of the time, there are a few beings here working on their own stuff and will buy a coffee or two during their stay. It's a holiday today, so maybe they decided to come in a bit later. There's a guy with tentacles who is usually early but often takes a nice day off.

This gray one looks at the chair for another moment before he shrugs. "Fine, I'll wait. I want a dozen."

"Sure, I'll mark it down and ring you up when they are ready." I jot down the order on a paper. "What's your name?"

He blinks, seemingly not wanting to tell me. But after another second, he says, "Vrek."

"Okay, I'll let you know." I put the note on the notice board. "Is there anything I can get you while you wait?"

He shakes his head and heads to the chairs. I head back to the kitchen, checking the online orders to make sure I have more than enough for everyone. Before the helper comes in, I should treasure the time and get more doughnuts ready.

Running a cafe in a city where most of the beings aren't humans is a bit more challenging than I expected. It took so long to convince them that the colorful doughnuts were harmless. Now that business has picked up, I'm a bit too booked up to my liking.

Boom or bust, boring.

I check the recipe again, making sure everything is going well. We have doughnuts here, and also bagels and other baked goods. I love making these and letting other beings know about nice food to try.

Sometimes, it's a bit scary to be almost the only human here. Everyone is bigger than me. The coal-gray guy is also bigger than me and he is very muscular. Heat sneaks up to my cheeks. He sends flame down my spine even though we barely talked. He's pretty handsome with long and curly light blonde hair and strong horns.

No, this isn't the time to think about that. He's just a customer and will be out of the door soon.

Chapter 2

Vrek

I sit on the chair, staring at the window and the beings outside the shop. I hate waiting. When a uzain wants something, they get it.

I fold my arms and pretend to be patient, just in case I'll scare that tiny human. She should be grateful I flew planets to be here. I heard that this cafe made good doughnuts, so when the crew had the time, I came here. But she made me wait.

That brown hair female walks around cleaning the counter and the insultingly empty doughnut trays.

She should only open the shop when she has stuff to sell me. This is such a waste of time.

I take a breath, trying to calm myself.

She annoys me. This cafe annoys me. There is soft music playing, which I hate. Humans are probably soft like marshmallows. I drum my fingers on the table as I check my phone with my other hand.

My team will be heading to another planet soon, and I better be there when we depart.

I narrow my eyes on that cute female. Somehow, she lights a fire in my stomach. The more I watch her walking around with a smile, the more... I want to grab her and kiss her. Maybe her lips are sweet like doughnuts, which I've never had before and can only imagine.

How would it feel if I pinned her against a wall...

I shake my head, trying my best to yank my mind off that. It isn't like I'm going to actually do it, so why even think about that?

Maybe my fleet isn't famous for kindness to others and we hunt villages and planets at times, but I'll never do something like that to a female. That's not honorable as a warrior.

She seems to be totally unaware of my mood.

It doesn't take long before she disappears from the storefront and back into the kitchen. Maybe she's finally going to bring me my doughnuts.

There are a few more beings around in the cafe; maybe these are the regulars here and they know when to show up for the doughnuts.

Interesting.

It takes a long wait, so much so it feels like a lifetime before she is out again. This time, she has a huge tray that smells amazingly well.

Now I'm hungry. Those must be doughnuts. I've heard of the food, but never thought about trying it before. But from what I see other beings talking about and all the reviews this place got, I'm curious.

She puts the tray into the large glass tank next to the counter. The doughnuts are pink with colorful sprinkles of something on them. I don't understand a thing about that, but those smell great and are teasing me.

She calls my name and I head over. She is moving the doughnuts into a pink paper box with a clamp. I head over to the counter, waiting for her to get the box ready.

She ties a bow with a ribbon and nudges the box forward for me. I take it and she asks, "How do you want to pay?"

Ah... Pay?

There are other beings around, so maybe I should pay. "With my card."

"Sure." She seems to be completely unaware.

I pull my card and swipe it, fighting myself to stop a groan. It has been so long since I paid for anything. When I want something, I just take it. But maybe I shouldn't do that when there are others around.

"Thank you. Hope you enjoy the doughnuts." She smiles and that...

My heart skips a beat and my cock twitches at that. That smile is a bit too tasty. I want her.

I pick up the box as she gestures for the next being to buy stuff from her. I wonder what's so amazing in the box.

I arrive at the tables again. Before I head back to the ship, maybe I should have a taste. I think I'm not supposed to rip the box. I carefully undo the bow and get a doughnut from the box.

It smells amazing.

I take a bite; it's soft with the sweet pink icing on it. The colorful sprinkles are also sweet. It's a soft and tasty doughnut, so much better than anything I've ever had on the spaceship. Soft and fluffy...

She is busy serving other beings, not looking in my direction. I take another bite of the doughnut. I think I know why everyone likes these. The doughnut almost melts in my mouth as I eat it.

She is going in and out of the kitchen all the time. Maybe she is the one operating the cafe and she is the one making these.

This doughnut is a bit too amazing. But if I'm leaving with just this dozen, and I already ate one... These are going to run out before I can blink.

Hmm...

Chapter 3

Serena

Finally, the last customer is gone and it is time to close down. My nice helper is already washing the utensils and tools in the kitchen.

We will finish washing everything, then take inventory just in case, and make sure we won't run out and can put in an order from the supplier.

My legs are sore and my arms are so tired that they feel like they might fall off my shoulders.

"I'll take the trash out," I announce to my helper as I pull the garbage bag and head to the backdoor of the cafe.

The robot that picks up trash will be coming soon and I don't want to miss that.

I tie a knot on the bag and kick the door open. It is dark out there. I shiver at the cooler wind outside. I hate this so much. but at the same time, I enjoy working in the cafe.

It's okay, I can tolerate the pain.

I put the garbage in the area marked with tape for the robot to collect. Maybe I can get a robot to do some of the work in the cafe, then it will be easier for me. But a robot will cost a ton upfront and I'm not sure—

Something moves and I jump backward. Are there stray animals living in the city? I've never seen one and—

I stumble as I step onto something behind me and I bump into something hard, but not hard enough to be the wall.

Before I can scream, a huge hand covers my mouth. What the fuck is happening?

I kick and bite the hand. I in no way look rich, why would someone kidnap me?

"Shut up!" That's an angry growl, which sounds familiar, as if I've heard that voice before, but...

While business is tough at times, I've never owed anyone any money. There's no reason—

A strong arm wraps around my neck and a spark of electricity spreads through my body. My body jerks so hard that everything in front of me shudders.

"Don't kill her, dumbass!" The angry growl is there again. There are at least two of them. Whoever planned this thinks I'd survive from even one of them?

I try to kick, but I can't even move. Something hits me again and everything turns black.

What is happening?

Chapter 4

Serena

Fuck...

My head hurts and so does my body. Where am I?

I close my eyes again because of the pain throbbing in my head. What happened?

It's cold here. I'm lying on something soft. My heart skips a beat and I push against the surface, sitting up.

I'm alone in a dark room. This is a huge bed, far bigger than mine. This place doesn't smell like my own.

I think someone kidnapped me when I took out the trash. I shiver at that. Who kidnapped me? Why?

Are these the notorious beings that sell other beings? Why me?

Not that I would ever hope this on others, but it makes no sense.

My heart hammers in my chest. It hurts and at the same time...

I sniff, finding tears running down my cheek. What's going to happen to me? I pull the blanket and ball up on myself, but the pain isn't ceasing. Will I die? What do these beings want from me?

There is a light click. Maybe someone is coming in. If I remain quiet, maybe they will think I'm asleep. This may not matter in the long term, but I can use every second I can get to figure out what's happening.

"She's still asleep." It's a male voice.

"I told you to be careful with her!" It's the same angry growl. Now that sounds like the coal-gray guy who was in the cafe early in the morning.

What's his name again?

Like...

Vrek.

Yes, that should be his name. Was he in the shop scouting and looking for a chance to kidnap me?

The first voice says, "Hey, it can't be that bad. Humans don't die that easily." But he soon screeches as if someone stepped on his toes, or worse.

Vrek growls, "Shut the fuck up! If she is injured, I'll have no end with you. Maybe you should go to your shift!"

The door closes. I peek out of the blanket when...

"I know you're awake," Vrek hisses. He comes over and grabs my hair, yanking me off the bed. "Were you eavesdropping?"

I shudder from his growl and it hurts my head when he grabs me like that. "Fuck... You've been growling like a moron."

"What?" He hisses right in my face. It's dark in the room, but I can recognize those horns and evil eyes. It is Vrek without a doubt.

"Put me down!"

"Don't tell me what to do," he snarls as if he's going to snap me in half.

I kick his stomach. But before I can reach him, he grabs my ankle, squeezing so hard that my eyes flood with tears. I grit my teeth as a groan fights to escape me. He must be wanting to see me in pain.

He smirks. "Look at you, struggling."

"You would love to see that, huh?" The pain is so strong that I'm shivering, but I hate to show it to him.

He drops me on the bed. "I won't say that. Are you feeling better now?"

I crash onto the bed. At least it is soft enough that I'm not hurt. Fire burns in my stomach, but I have to wait for a chance.

He folds his arms as he watches me. "When I ask you a question, you answer."

Maybe I would have, but he kidnapped me and expected me to cooperate, so that's not going to happen, ever. I look away from him.

"I said, answer me."

Except I refuse. I won't even talk to him if he keeps hurting me.

He grabs my throat and glares at me with his red eyes that shoot fire at me. I grit my teeth, refusing to show a hint of fear.

He runs his finger along my cheeks. "Feisty, huh?"

I hate that. His touch sends shivers down my spine.

He puts me down again. "You're lucky I decided to leave you alive."

I huff but stop myself before I'll end up talking to him.

He leans over again. "Look, you are here to make doughnuts for me and the fleet."

I'm what?

He rests his hands on his waist. "Are you listening?"

I roll my eyes. This must be a joke. I don't have time to waste with him. I have to be back at my place and get ready for the next day's work.

I get off the bed and head to the door. He hisses. "Where're you going?"

"Back home."

He laughs. "Do you think I'm just going to stand here and watch you leave?"

I turn around and glare at him. "You kidnapped me."

He smirks, seemingly proud of that. "Yes, I did a clean job with that. There's no going back home. We aren't even on that planet now."

Fuck...

"Where are we?"

"In space, flying."

Fuck...

He comes closer and lowers his head; maybe he's trying to show off his horns and threaten me with those. "It is time to accept your fate."

My fate? "And what's that? Are you looking to sell me off to someone?"

He smirks. "I have something in mind that will benefit me more. Your fate is to keep making me doughnuts, like I've already said."

I fold my arms. "No, I'm not going to do that."

"What?" he growls, and I fight not to shiver. "I said you're going to make doughnuts."

"And I said you can't make me do anything." I fold my arms.

He'd crazy to kidnap me for doughnuts. I bet there is an actual reason.

"I don't care. You're here now, and that means you're mine."

I roll my eyes. If that's the case, I guess he should learn to ask nicely. Not that I even want to stay here, let alone do anything for him. "No, I'm not yours. Never. You kidnapped me. My employee will soon report you and save me."

He laughs. My cheeks heat up and I have to try my best to keep my eyes on him. He is still laughing, and his smirk annoys me. But he's a bit too tall for me to punch in the face. So, I guess I'll have to wait for a better chance.

He is still laughing, so much so that he's shaking.

I grit my teeth. Maybe he is laughing so hard that he won't even see me. I sneak up to his back. He doesn't turn around, so I kick his ass as hard as I can.

He stumbles forward, but not enough to fall on his face. Before I can blink, he is at my throat and he yanks me up to face him, since I'm a lot shorter than him. "What did you do?"

I snort out a laugh. "Kick your ass, duh."

"How dare you?"

"What are you going to do about it?"

He flings me to the bed. My face hits the pillow and there are stars in my head for a moment. The bed shakes when he climbs onto it. I turn around, but before I can, he plants his huge hand on the back of my neck and he pins me down, shoving my face into the pillow.

I can't breathe and he doesn't seem to care.

He bites my earlobe, and that sends a spark through my body. "If I were you, I'd be smarter. Do as I say and it will benefit you."

I remain quiet, not knowing what to do. I know I shouldn't have kicked him, but I don't regret it. If he's going to kill me, at least I tried to avenge myself.

He lets go of me. I remain on the bed, trying my best to not move. He waits for another second, also in silence. I have all the patience in the world when I have nothing else to do.

He pokes my back, but I remain quiet. He grunts. "Are you dead?"

Does he seriously think that I'm going to answer? That's such a stupid question.

The bed moves again, but I doubt he will leave me alone just like that. Maybe he's just trying to fool me.

It doesn't take long before he pokes my back again. "I know you aren't dead. Get up."

I wait for another moment, not knowing what's in his head.

He pokes me again. "Or, maybe you like my bed a bit too much."

Fuck him...

He yanks me up with his hand on my clothes. "Stop pretending to be dead."

I roll my eyes at that. "You can kill me and make me actually dead."

"Not now. But if you keep defying me, I'll kill you."

"Oh yeah?"

"I've burned down villages and destroyed outposts, so if you want to have a taste of that, I don't mind." He points at his horns. "Look at these. I won't mind showing you what I can do with them."

"What year is this? You still fight with horns like an animal?"

"What the fuck!"

"And you are here huffing and puffing like an idiot. You can't even talk like a normal being."

He should be mad, but he smirks at me again. "You're interesting. Now, you should get to work." He picks me up and holds me under his arm, making it look easy. I kick and scream, but that doesn't seem to bother him.

He heads to the door and gets into the corridor. I wince because it's a lot brighter out here. He pats my head. "You're going to make me nice doughnuts."

So... He was serious about that? Fuck... I didn't figure I could get into trouble just by being decently good at baking.

He isn't wearing shoes. I didn't pay attention before, but this is weird.

He walks and seems to be humming a song under his breath. He is a bit too giddy. Maybe he's happy that he has me here, thinking I'm just going to cave in.

"Oh, this is the human?" Someone else says.

I lift my head to see another coal-gray male. There are swirls and markings on his chest. Maybe there are the same ones on Vrek's chest, too.

Hm... so these beings walk around half-naked. The male in front of me has a belt with a laser gun and other tools. He's wearing baggy trousers, and looks like a slacker. Vrek looks equally dumb, if not even dumber.

Vrek says, "Yes, this is the one who made the dough-nuts I brought to the ship."

"Ah, is she going to make more?"

"I'll make her make more."

The male watches me and licks his lips. At least they are talking about doughnuts, otherwise... It isn't a good sign when someone watches you and licks their lips.

The male nods. "Sure, I can't wait."

I start moving again. Vrek carries me around as if I'm a suitcase or something. I'm not his property and he doesn't get to do that to me. So much for imagining that I'll make doughnuts for him.

Vrek says as he makes me turn a corner, "Look, every-one's waiting."

"That's not my problem. No wonder you hesitated when I asked how you were going to pay. You never thought of paying."

"Yes, when I want something, I take it."

That is some crazy talk right there. "You're a fucking robber."

"Oh, we're warriors, don't be silly." He presses a but-ton and a door slides open. "You'll be working here." He finally puts me down.

This is a pretty big kitchen with a big kitchen island in the center. At a glance, they have every piece of equipment I could need. There are big stoves and big pots, probably for cooking for everyone all at once.

He sneers and towers over me. "The guys are taking a break before they prepare breakfast, so you are here to make doughnuts as snacks. There should be enough time for that."

So... This is the middle of the night?

I fold my arms and lean on the kitchen island. "No, I'm not going to do anything for you."

He cracks his knuckles. "Are you sure about that?"

I shrug. "Yeah, and sadly, you can't force me. If I get hurt, I won't be able to make any doughnuts."

He sucks in a deep breath. "You aren't going to cooperate."

"No! You kidnapped me! I don't want to be here. I have my own business, and you took everything from me." A surge of tears threaten to escape me, but I hate to let him see that. "I won't even ask you to send me home, knowing you won't."

He grunts and mutters something under his breath. "You are here to stay."

I look away from him. I don't want to be here on a stupid spaceship and stay with a crazy male. Except I'm not sure how I can get out of here. If I was on a spaceship and they're flying... That makes it hard.

Chapter 5

Vrek

I glare at the tiny human in front of me. She should be scared, but she is clearly not even intimidated. Is there something wrong with my horns?

She looks away from me as if I'm something dirty that she despises. Does she think I'll be scared of her?

I hiss at her again. "I can always punish you."

She glances at me with cold eyes. "I don't doubt it. You can do that, but you'll be getting further away from your doughnuts."

How dare she think she can threaten me with that?

"I can always get another being to make me dough-nuts."

"So why don't you do that already?" She huffs and stares at the pots and stoves in front of her, still ignoring my glare.

This is the first time someone has dared to defy me like that. I don't allow that. She should understand...

There's heat in my stomach. I want her. The more she tries to fight back, the more she lights the fire inside me.

I'm good at destroying resistance, but with her... I'm not sure what I should do.

I've never felt this with anyone else, but I want to hold her in my arms and kiss her. But that's so different from what I'm used to doing.

Maybe I want her for more than the doughnuts she makes, but I'm not going to show it. She should learn a lesson.

I say, "If you start now, you can have breakfast."

She laughs, and that sends my blood boiling. She folds her arms. "I don't care for your food. You didn't even let me sleep through the night, and you want me to work for you, unpaid and threatened. I don't know which planet you come from, but that's not how it works."

So she expects me to pay her? "Stop daydreaming. You are here to work like a slave for me."

She snorts and ignores me, still not moving a step to start working on my doughnuts.

I grab her throat, glaring into her eyes. She shivers, but she scowls back at me, certain that I won't dare to hurt her.

I lean closer. Maybe I kind of like her and she makes the fire in my stomach confusing, but that doesn't mean she can get things her way. This is a uzaine ship, not a human ship.

She comes closer to me, but she is shaking and she isn't hiding it as well as she tries. She stands on her tiptoes, but still not tall enough to be up against me. She jabs her finger at my chest as if she is in charge.

"Look, that's not the right way to ask for doughnuts."

I lift my brows at her. The closer she gets to me, the stronger the fire grows in me. The flame spreads along the markings on my chest. Those are swirls I'm born with, and what every member of my species has. I take a deep breath, taking in her sweet scent. She's almost as good as the doughnuts she can make.

There's a strong urge in me to pin her down and tell her who's the one in charge, but I stop myself when she pokes my chest harder with her finger.

She says, "I'm not going to give you anything until you learn to respect me."

Respect her? This tiny human who I took and put on the ship? I snort out a laugh. "Stop dreaming. You're just a human and you're here to work. I'll give you time to think about it and accept your fate. Now back to my room."

She rolls her eyes and doesn't move a single step. I grab the back of her neck and make her walk. She's testing me, and I'm going to make her submit.

After I toss that human female into my room, I get outside in the corridor to clear my head. She drives me crazy for some reason. I should grab her throat and threaten her some more, but...

It can't be her words that hold me back. There's nothing stopping me.

Maybe I don't want to break her, that won't help my goal.

"Vrek." A fellow waves at me.

"Yes, what's up?"

"The Captain is looking for you."

My heart skips a beat. That may or may not be a good thing. "What's it about?"

He shrugs. "I don't know. But I guess it's about the female. You said she can make us doughnuts, right?"

I nod. "Yes, she made the ones we had earlier."

I hate how everyone here has a sensitive nose, and my box of doughnuts disappeared quicker than I could blink. At least I managed to grab another bite for myself.

I fucking paid for the thing. And these monsters —

Fine, they are my kind and my fleet, and it isn't like I've never taken their stuff either. We take each others' things, or as some other beings say, we share. I shudder at the word. That's not my favorite word at all.

He licks his lips. "Is she working already?"

"Taking a rest for now."

"Ah, okay. I can't wait. You better get going to the Captain."

I nod and hurry to the control panel. Captain is always there, even when it isn't his shift. This isn't my shift, and therefore I had time to spend with the female.

The path to the control panel seems to be a lot shorter than I remembered. I press the button to get into the control room. Everyone on shift is working, so no one looks over to me. Captain is sitting on his seat on the elevated platform. He stares out the window, deep in his thoughts.

I take a breath, hoping I didn't interrupt him. There are clicking sounds of the others typing and checking the system alongside a few beeps here and there from the machines. My heartbeat sounds loud in my ears.

Captain remains quiet for awhile before he turns around to me, acknowledging my existence.

I bow my head to him. "Captain, you were looking for me?"

He nods. He is a strong uzaine with a lot of combat experience and fabulous horns. "Yes, about the female." He looks at the ones working and stands. "We'll talk in the strategy room."

I take a step back as he gets out of his seat. In addition to our uniform, Captain also has his black cape on. He only takes that off when we go into battle, so he doesn't stick out as the leader of our group to any attackers.

He heads out of the control panel and presses the button for the strategy room that's close by, a large room with a long table and chairs. It's a boring but important place. He leans on the wall close to the door, so I remain standing, keeping my distance from him.

"Vrek, how's the female doing?"

"She is... getting used to the ship."

He muses with a serious face. "You see, there's a reason we don't allow females on the ship."

"But you know that she can make great doughnuts." I'm still bitter about how he got a whole doughnut for himself, but he is the captain, so I'll just have to bear with that.

He taps his horns. "I understand. You better get her working soon enough, otherwise..." He watches me with cold eyes. He is serious about the rules, and I don't dare to challenge him.

"Yes, Captain." I bow my head, avoiding looking into his eyes.

"I hope it will work out well. I like the doughnuts. Can I trust you to handle that?"

"Yes, Captain, don't worry about it. I'll make the human behave and work for us."

"Good. Now, you can go back and enjoy your time off."

"Thank you, Captain."

I move to the side for him to leave. When he is gone, it feels like I can finally breathe again. Captain is a great warrior everyone respects and secretly fears, and I'm one of them.

How long do I have to convince the female? For some reason that I can't point my horns at, I don't want to let go of her. I knew it when I grabbed her in the alley. There's something in me that screams how she is meant for me.

Captain may not like that. No females are allowed on our ship so no one will be distracted. I know the rules and have never thought I would be the one treading the line, but...

Maybe Captain also wants doughnuts enough that he will give this a chance. I can only hope his good mood continues.

Chapter 6

Serena

I sit on the bed, staring at the door after Vrek tossed me into his room and closed the door.

So, he thinks that he can make me do stuff for him just by sneering and threatening me. And offering to give me breakfast if I do as he wishes?

I snort out a laugh, even though he isn't here. Maybe I should be scared of such a tall and muscular guy, but something about him shouts that he isn't going to hurt me regardless of what I do.

It's strange to feel that way, but the way he looks at me...

How would it feel if he grabbed me in his arms?

Not in an intimidating or forceful way, but just...

If we met each other without this kidnapping craziness, maybe it would be different. I shrug. It isn't like I'd care about a crazy male. His horns look nice, but that's pretty much it.

I let out a sigh. I suppose I should destroy his room or make a mess out of it so he will learn to respect me. But I'm so tired that I don't even want to move anymore.

Maybe my body is coming down from the high when he and I glared at each other. Maybe I got used to it by facing troublesome customers. Some of them are similar in size to Vrek, causing me trouble in similar ways.

I hate that even when I stand on my tiptoes, he's still taller than me and can still tower over me. I flex and move my feet. If only I were a bit taller, maybe he would know his place.

But I just want to crawl into a ball and cry.

I pull up the blanket, covering my face. This is a big bed for beings his size, so that makes for a lot of room to roll around.

Now that Vrek kidnapped me here, I doubt I'm going back to my old life again. While I don't enjoy the rough day-to-day at times, it isn't that bad. I want to be there for the customers and to stay in my own home. I don't want to be here with ugly-ass huge guys telling me what to do.

I want to be back in my own cafe, even if that means I have to make the dough myself and wash all the utensils. I shiver as tears fall along my cheeks. I wipe my face with the blanket, but the tears keep coming.

I hate him. If I told him to leave in the morning or he left without coming back and buying doughnuts from me, maybe I wouldn't have gotten into this mess.

Why?

I'm just a human trying to survive and make a living with something I enjoy, is it that wrong?

"Where are you hiding?"

A growl echoes through the room, and I flinch under the blanket. Did he not see me? Or maybe he's trying to scare me.

The blanket is gone. I'm on the bed, alone, and it feels like I'm naked even though I'm clothed.

He smirks. "Here you are."

I close my eyes, waiting for him to yank me off the bed. He's already done that a bit too many times.

But nothing happens.

The bed shudders as he climbs onto it. His hand is on my back, but he is gently patting me instead of smacking.

I remain quiet, waiting for him to morph back into the monster that just screamed and shouted threats.

"Female. Wait. What's your name?"

So he's interested in my name now? Not just trying to grab me and toss me to the kitchen?

He hisses when I say nothing and holds onto me tightly before answering. "I said, what's your name? Unless you want to be called female all the time."

Is he trying to be kind, thinking I'd bite and I'd do as he wishes? After he has been a monster, he thinks that I should be grateful and behave to repay his kindness. I'm not that dumb. This is insulting.

He lets out a low growl. "Talk to me and stop pretending to be dead."

"Serena. And your name is trashy jerk."

He sucks in a breath, seemingly sucking in all the air in the room. "You know my name."

"Trashy ass. Bastard."

"You hate me." He tickles my side and I turn around and sneer at him. He smirks. "Look at this angry face."

"I pity your sad ass. You can't even get a nice doughnut without using force. Well, to be accurate, you can't even get doughnuts with force. Because I'm not making them."

He glares at me and I shiver from the inside. My blood seems to be freezing, but I refuse to back off from the staring contest.

He reaches to my chin and I slap his hand away from me. He huffs. "Listen, I'm trying to treat you better."

"Except I'm not a pet. And I'm not going to think that you're actually a nice guy after you kidnapped me and forced me to be on your stinky ugly spaceship. You are the one who yanked me away from my life. I'm never going to forgive you and I'm never going to do anything for you."

He blinks, like he didn't anticipate that. "Look, I'm trying to make it easier on you. If you keep acting like this, Captain is going to be mad."

"Oh yeah? I don't even care. Kill me, sell me, do whatever to me, you bastard."

He pulls away and tilts his head to the side. "You're interesting."

I fold my arms. I hate this. "Where's the spaceship going?"

He shrugs. "I have no idea. The captain decides where we go."

"So you're just a useless body existing on this ship."

He sneers again, his lips quivering as he tries to control himself. "I'm not useless."

I shrug. "Feels like that. Nothing's in your control, you just exist. And maybe that's the reason you feel so good bullying someone like me who isn't trained to fight. Such a weakling."

He huffs and puffs, but maybe he is self-conscious enough to control himself, not wanting to fall right into my description of him.

"Serena, listen. It will only benefit you if you work with me."

This is laughable.

He continues, "If you refuse to work for us, Captain won't be nice to you."

I shrug. "I have nothing to lose. You've taken my life away from me, along with all my choices. I don't care. If he wants me dead, he can just do it. Wasn't he the one who told you to kidnap me?"

He shakes his head. "Not exactly."

"So... you kidnapped me on your own. Hm..." I smirk. Maybe he isn't as smart as he seemed to be. "You need this to work out so you won't be laughed at, right?"

He hisses but says nothing. Maybe I'm right about that.

I'm upset with my lost life and everything I've built for myself. But there's nothing I can do to go back there, so...

I poke his chest. "Maybe you're the one who has to work with me if you don't want to be the laughing stock. That's not something you can solve by killing me or even selling me."

He glares at my hand, probably fighting his urge to slap it off him. But it looks like I'm getting the situation under control. After all, I'm using a brain instead of big muscles, which is all he has.

He lifts my chin with a smirk. "If you think this is your chance to take charge, you're dead wrong."

"But there's nothing else you can do to me. You're the one with your reputation at stake, if you even have one."

"You love to annoy me." His smirk grows. Did I miss something?

He holds my side and pulls me to his lap. My heart races, but there is heat in my stomach. This is weird. But at the same time, I wonder what he's planning.

I ask, "What are you trying to do?"

"Make you sit on my lap and make you behave."

"Is that part of your attempt to please me?"

He grunts, and his hot breath lands on my neck.

I turn around on his lap. "What's the plan again? Do you think I'm a pet or something, and you can stroke me some and be done with it?"

"That's not what I've been thinking. You need to understand that I'm just here to help you."

"Good cop, bad cop? Just because your captain may be a disgusting being, doesn't mean you're any better than him. I'm not going to pick one of you and imagine either is going to help me."

He sucks in a deep breath. "All we want is doughnuts."

"Then you'll have to work for that."

His eyes widen, and he stares at me, as if he isn't sure whether he heard my words right.

I pat his chest again. If he thinks his little trick is going to work, he's dead wrong. "Look, maybe you should start pleasing me and maybe I will make you some doughnuts. Otherwise, imagine what the others will say. That you can't even get doughnuts, despite kidnapping me."

He grunts. "You have to keep mentioning that."

"Yes, you already owed me a ton when you forced me to be here, so you better start making up for that." It's interesting how he seems to be quieter now. Maybe he figures out there's nothing he can do to me.

He sighs. "So, what do you want? And you're the one patting me as if I'm a pet."

"I'm hungry."

His eyes darken on me. Maybe I didn't say the right thing. I swallow as the heat in my stomach grows even stronger.

He asks, "What do you mean? You better be clear. What are you hungry for?"

His cock twitches. He probably doesn't mean it, but when he made me sit on his lap...

Heat streams to my cheeks and I look away. "Hungry for actual food."

"Not my meat."

Does he seriously think that I'll want to fuck him? I snarl at him. "Fuck, no! Maybe you pulled me on your lap, thinking I'd want you, but don't you give yourself too much credit."

But there is a pulse between my legs, making it tempting to let him hold me.

No.

I move away from him and sit on the bed instead. "Maybe you should go and grab me breakfast. I want bacon and toast with butter."

He shows off his horns again, but I ignore his threats. I add, "And also coffee, with cream."

"Well, we don't have coffee here."

That's such a bummer. "Tea?"

"Not sure if humans would like our tea."

"I'll decide, so bring it here. And also honey for tea."

He sucks in a deep breath, puffing his muscular chest. "Now, you're telling me what to do."

"Yes. And are you going to do it?"

He folds his arms and watches me with a death glare. "If you dare to mess with me, I'm going to have no end with you."

He leaves, huffing and puffing with rage. I watch his back with a smile. Serena, one. Meathead, zero.

Chapter 7

Vrek

I hate this. That female, Serena, huh? She thinks that she can grab my horns and make me do stuff for her.

I want my doughnuts, and I don't want to be the laughingstock. She isn't completely off base, but at the same time, I hate that. There's no way she should be able to read me like that.

I arrive at the food area, suck in a breath, and take in the scent of tasty food. There are others getting breakfast already. In order to not look dumb to be only fetching food for a tiny human, I also grab food for myself. And she wants things off the menu, that's going to get me looks...

She drives me crazy. But at the same time, she brings a smile to my face. I wasn't thinking about that earlier, but I want her even more. It's not just about doughnuts. The longer she's near me, the more I want her.

The hum in my stomach is so strong. And when I had her on my lap, it was so tempting. And when she casually said she was hungry...

It would be nice if she wanted my cock. I could fuck her enough that she'll learn her place.

I want her... A human female... Interesting.

I get my food and head back to my room, ignoring what others may think of me to have two sets of food. I open the door to my room. She is sitting on the bed, watching me with those sneakily naughty eyes and that smirk...

She smiles. "Looks like you're getting yourself something too. Still haven't admitted defeat?"

"Defeat? From what? You?" I laugh, even though it hurts my stomach to hear that. Even this tiny human is laughing at me.

She licks her lips, and I would much rather kiss those lips and make her my breakfast. I put the tray on the table to the side. "If you want the food, you will come here." Ha, I have an idea. "And I'll feed you."

Her eyes snap open. "What did you say?"

"You will come here and I'll feed you breakfast." I smirk. It isn't like I'll ever think of her as a pet, but if she hates that, it's exactly what I'll do.

"Now you're the one who wants to fuck with me."

I grin as I watch her make her way to me. After getting off the bed, she looks smaller and a bit shorter. I pat her head when she is in front of me.

"Fuck!" I yell as she knees me right in the balls. I'm good at tolerating pain, but this... Pain spreads fully through me, but I refuse to hunch and show more pain than I have to.

She snickers. "I dare you do that again."

"Feisty, aren't we." I straighten, still biting the inside of my mouth to fight the pain. "If you're asking for a fight, I can give you that." How dare she?

She takes a fork, lifting it to me. "That's your lesson. If you want to treat me like a pet, you're going to regret it."

No one has ever done this to me. I won't allow this to happen. I snatch her throat, but she ducks away from me. She must think she's smart.

She goes under my arm to my back, but I take a step back and ram into her. She stumbles backward. Before she can regain balance, I dash forward and pin her to the ground. I grab her ankle, pushing that to her side.

I hiss at her. "I've warned you. You're the one choosing violence."

She grits her teeth, refusing to back off. "You are the one starting it."

Oh yeah? I'm going to—

My stomach rumbles and she chuckles. I hiss. She better shut up, otherwise...

She says, "Maybe we should eat. That may help your poor stomach."

"And maybe I'll decide not to eat you." I let go of her. I'm hungry and she's lucky.

I pat the chair. "Sit."

She rolls her eyes, getting up from the floor quicker than I expected. "No. Stop telling me what to do."

"Don't you dare to think you'd be equal to me."

"If you want your doughnuts, I better be, if not above you a tad bit."

This fucking human! I clench my fist, glaring at her. She's lucky I want my doughnuts. I hate it when someone threatens me.

She says, "It would have been a lot easier if you started out asking nicely without kidnapping me. You are the one making it hard. I'm not going to be sorry for you, not a tiny bit."

I suck a breath. "After I eat, you'll regret it."

She moves to the table and takes my plate. I'm about to hiss at her when she puts my plate on the table, then takes the tray with her and goes to the other side of the table.

She chew on a piece of bacon, enjoying it with a smile. I hate her.

I grab my bread roll and chew on it. It's a nice and thick piece of bread baked with nuts, and rolled with roasted meat and gravy. I'm hungry and glad it's still warm despite the lesson I had to teach her, which... I don't think I was that successful, sadly.

She downs another strip of bacon. I like bacon. It's finely spiced meat that we got from humans with our loot from another village we visited a while ago. The way she eats it and licks the fork tempts me. She's asking for trouble with that cute face. I want to make her scream, but I don't want to hurt her.

Now, she picks up the cup of tea, sniffing and blowing it. She takes a sip and adds honey.

It's not that my food is bad, but she makes the bacon look tasty. I can't take my eyes away from her, but she seems to ignore my gaze.

Or maybe she is scared and avoiding me. That sounds better.

I take another bite, enjoying the spicy gravy and the nicely roasted meat.

She sips her tea with a smile before she moves to the toast. She takes a bite, but scowls. "Hey, is this thing toast? Are you messing with me?"

I straighten and sneer. "Yes, that's toast, are you blind?"

She puts it down with an even deeper scowl. "And your kind made it here on the spaceship?"

"Yeah, the kitchen crew made it. What's your problem?"

"Geez, no wonder you love my doughnuts so much that you decided to kidnap me." She moves over to me and glances at my food. "Look at this. Do you eat this all the time?"

I nod. "Yes, this is good food."

She moves away with her brows scrunched together. She takes a piece of the bread roll and chews on it. "Now I pity you. I don't even understand why. Do they secretly hate you or something? This is hard like a rock. Is that on purpose?"

I take a breath. "Come on, it isn't that bad."

She moves closer and sniffs at my food. "At least the gravy smells nice. Maybe the meat is good."

I narrow my eyes on her. "As if you can top that."

She blinks. "It's tempting to fix everything you can't seem to figure out. But maybe you're setting this up to make me start working."

"I swear I'm not. This is the regular food we have."

"I guess I'll want a steak for my lunch and dinner. Maybe you like your bread this way, but not me."

Is she insulting my taste and our food?

She goes back to her tray and sips on the tea, not interested in the toast anymore. I hiss at her. "Don't waste food."

"But it's so bad. It's already hot and fresh, but if it's supposed to be bread, this isn't it. It can be a chopping board, though. Stone hard." She taps the toast.

I smirk. "My cock is pretty hard too."

She huffs and laughs. "Are you trying to flirt with me? Keep that hard-on to yourself, silly."

I thought she would be mad, but she wasn't. Interesting. The flame in my stomach is there again, and the heat pulses through my body in ways different than when I'm with other beings. I want her.

But this isn't the time for that.

I clear my throat and swallow my food. I don't understand what's wrong with this. The gravy is a good match with the bread. Maybe she's just messing with me. I finish my food and down my glass of water.

She is watching me with raised eyebrows.

I ask, "What's with that look?"

"It must be a miracle you can finish this kind of food."

I roll my eyes at that. "All you can make is doughnuts."

"Good ones, so good that you couldn't resist yourself."

I hate her. "And you aren't proving your value when you aren't making anything."

"I'm not going to make anything for someone who doesn't know what respect is. I don't have to prove anything to anyone."

That's the one thing we may never agree on. Maybe she will learn, soon. Very soon.

I fold my arms. "So, you had food. Are you going to start working?"

"Nope." She smirks. "Now, you should show me around the spaceship and tell me more about your fleet."

Does she think she gets to interview me?

She tilts her head to the side. "Do you have to make it hard? If you want us to work together, you're going to be a decent being and stop wanting to be on top of me all the time."

I go to her and lift her chin. "Look, when I'm on top of you, you'll be happy."

She pats my chest. "Who knows? You are so confident."

"I am. I know I'm good."

She makes my cock twitch, and I might just explode from the heat inside me. I stroke her cheek. "Can I hug you?"

She lifts her brows, seemingly surprised. "Well, yes, you can."

I wrap my arms around her and pull her to my chest. Fuck... Maybe I shouldn't have done this. Her soft body is so tempting. I...

She chuckles and pats my back. "I wonder what's on your mind. Are you going to show me around?"

I hate how I'm playing right into her hand, but maybe that's what I'll do for now. Not sure how long the captain is willing to wait and for some reason, I don't want to lose her.

"Yes, I will, but you have to behave."

She laughs but says nothing. I hold her tight for another moment before letting go. Maybe what I feel is just because I've been away from any female for a long time. Probably not something I have to care about.

Chapter 8

Serena

Finally, Vrek isn't sneering and growling at me. Maybe he's learned to treat me well and mean it.

He's walking ahead of me, seemingly still mad at me. Can't blame him when he thinks that he's golden with those muscles.

My cheeks are still hot from his tight hug. His body is burning hot. Maybe I shouldn't have let him hold me. But I was curious enough. At least his muscles were good to cuddle with, probably the only use of that meathead.

There are also black swirls on his back, like how there is on his chest. Do they mean anything? Maybe these guys have unique markings, like fingerprints.

"I'm telling you," he says with his hands on his waist. "You are the tiny human here."

"In terms of size? I don't doubt that."

He grunts. Is he trying again? Must he always feel better and feel more important than me? I thought we'd come to the conclusion that it is better for us to respect each other. Maybe I should have kicked his balls harder.

I've already kicked his ass, and his balls, but somehow, he still wants to flex.

He says, "You should learn your place."

"Seriously? I thought we've gone through that already, Vrek."

He halts at a corner and I almost bump into him. I'm about to complain and punch his back when he bows at that side of the corner.

I take a step back. Within seconds, another big coal-gray male comes around. He must be the one turning the corner, so Vrek halted.

This one has even stronger horns. He has a black cape and he wears boots, unlike Vrek with his bare feet. He gives me a nod. "This is the female."

Vrek answers, "Yes, Captain."

Captain. No wonder this one looks like he is someone important, and no wonder Vrek seems tense.

Captain gives a faint nod, his face is steel and his gaze can stab through me. "What is she doing here?"

Vrek says, "I'm showing her around."

I fold my arms. "Maybe you're the one who wanted to kidnap me here."

Vrek turns to look at me, but he isn't sneering. His eyes scream how I should regret what I've said.

Captain smirks. "Interesting. No, I'm not the one with that idea. Vrek wanted that to happen, and I allowed it."

I shrug. "I don't care. You're the captain, so everything happening is your fault."

Captain folds his arms. "Feisty there. Maybe someone should teach you how to talk better."

Vrek says, "Sorry, Captain. I haven't had the time to introduce her to everything. I was meant to send her to the kitchen and get her working, so..."

Captain shrugs. "That's not the problem. Female, I'll let this slide, but if you dare to do this again, you'll regret it. I'm not Vrek, and I don't care about doughnuts."

Oh... if that's the case, I won't have enough cards in my hands to play against this one.

He continues, "If you are proven to be of no use to us, you'll be gone. You may not like my way, but you won't have a choice."

My blood freezes in me. Captain's gaze is a lot sharper than Vrek's, and I know better than to mess with him. Not until I figure out this place and all the beings here.

Captain looks at me for another moment. "I mean my words. Human, be smart with your life." He continues down his path. I turn around, sticking my tongue out at his back.

There is a low hiss next to me. Vrek covers his mouth and stares at me with wide eyes. Maybe he's holding back a smile. I lift my brow at him.

When Captain probably is far enough away, I say, "Looks like that's something you've been wanting to do. But a bit too timid to."

He groans. "Geez, you haven't learned a single thing. Everyone respects the captain."

"Maybe. But that doesn't mean you've never thought about that. Maybe you should treat me better." I wink at him.

He sucks a deep breath. "Let's go to the kitchen."

"Are you trying to make me work?"

He scowls and looks to where Captain disappears. "You heard him."

Is the captain that scary? Or... "Every one of you on this ship is going to coax me into doing stuff for you. Your captain and you are just cooperating."

"Well, we are a team, so we are going to be working on the same goal. But he means his word. Maybe I won't hurt you, but he won't care."

"This is exactly what I mean. You pretend to be the nice guy and he will be the bad one, then you pretend to be helping me. It's just the same. You're just trying to make me listen to you."

He groans. "You are a dummy, huh? Yes, that's what I want to do, but it doesn't mean he's pretending. Why don't you just cooperate a bit more?"

How dare he say something like that? He should know. Is he pretending to be innocent or is he really clueless?

I poke his chest. He grabs my hand but doesn't squeeze. I take my hand back. "Are you really clueless as to why I won't make anything for you? Maybe it's time for us to be honest with each other."

He rubs his horn. "Well, you mentioned that I kidnapped you and you don't seem to like that."

I click my tongue. "Exactly."

"I will punch you if you refuse."

"And that's supposed to work? I thought you already knew that's not going to work on me. I'd kick your balls every chance I get."

He flinches for a second. "Well... I already brought you breakfast. But you don't seem to be satisfied."

"Do you remember how you threatened not to let me eat?"

He grunts and sneers, seemingly lacking words.

I take a step closer to him. "Did you think your threat would work on me?"

He grunts. "If I put my heart into it and beat you up, no one will care. Are you up to give that a try?" He flexes his strong arms. With those muscles, I have no doubt he can crush me.

I hold up my hand between us. "Look, if I get injure d..."

He smirks. "We have healing equipment. I can break you over and over until you learn your place."

I swallow with my throat tight. I know that there is equipment for that. There are a lot of those in hospitals, and for beings who are always flying, I won't doubt they have them on their ships.

"Maybe that will heal me up, but it won't be the same anymore. Do you even understand doughnuts?"

"I understand enough to eat them. And I understand that if you will never make me some, I won't have to worry or care."

Now, that's what I don't need. He doesn't need to think about that. Messing around with him is fun, but at the same time, I should get better at making him behave my way; just like what he is trying to do, but in reverse.

I take a step back. "Look, we just have to come to an agreement."

"You aren't in a place to negotiate." He is standing right in front of me and his eyes are dark. His cock twitches and his trousers aren't hiding it well.

My cheeks flush red at once and I look away. What is he even thinking about?

He follows my gaze and the smirk on his face grows. "What are you looking at?"

"At whether someone's coming."

"Hmm..." He turns over to look; maybe he is confused, or just simple-minded. "No one is coming."

"Yeah." I shrug. "I was thinking maybe you wouldn't want others to see me poking your chest."

He rubs his chin. "Interesting. Anyway, tell me, what'll get you working?"

"It's not that hard. You treat me as an equal like the rest of your fleet. I know the captain is above you guys, and I can accept that. But no more threatening me."

He takes in a deep breath. "Seriously?"

"Doughnuts?"

He blinks. "Well, you know what Captain is going to do to you if you keep acting like a brat."

"And you'll be the laughing stock for failing to make me cooperate. I'm already offering you kindness. I'm not sure why you'd think threatening me is going to work. Maybe that's how you're used to doing things, but it's time to change that for me."

He lets out a low growl. "Never."

"Doughnuts?"

He narrows his eyes on me. "You can stay in my room and warm my bed, and that's it. I can still find use out of you, whether you like it or not."

"Maybe you'll be the one warming my bed."

The way he looks at me makes me regret my words at once.

He laughs. "Yes, I'll keep you warm with these arms."

Fuck...

Maybe I should be mad, just like how I should have when he teased me. But there are tingles between my legs and I hate that. The warmth in me surges again, as if his arms are going to solve that.

But no.

I'm not going to get close with this bastard who kidnapped me and made me negotiate the stupidest thing ever.

I hiss. "Go away. No one wants your stupid arms."

He wriggles his fingers at me. "You'll learn to enjoy me very soon. For now, let's move on to doughnuts."

Except that's not going to happen, no way. I need him to be thinking about something else.

"You haven't agreed to anything. You'll treat me as an equal for doughnuts."

"I'll agree after I see the doughnuts."

I narrow my eyes at him. It looks like he and I have very different views about how the world works.

He grunts and he moves his hand over my head. If he dares to pat me, maybe he needs a reminder with a kick at his balls.

Right before he touches my hair and I destroy his balls, his hand stops.

"Serena, you are so interesting."

Maybe he's never run into someone who will defy him and isn't scared of him.

"I'll be even more interesting if you listen to me a bit and do as I offered. Doughnuts, and respect."

"Fine, I can do that. Doughnuts first, but if you decide to be a brat again, I won't let it slide."

"Deal." Did I win?

Chapter 9

Vrek

Serena puts the mixing bowl and the tools on the kitchen island. Maybe she's finally going to make me doughnuts.

I glance at the door of the kitchen, hoping no one will come here. This is an off hour, no one should be here. There's a small window on the door, which has no peeking heads for now.

"What are you waiting for? Get me the ingredients." Serena points at the cupboards. "Do you think I'll know where things are?"

I straighten from the stove counter. "What do you need?"

"Here." She gives me a list which she spent a few minutes scribbling down. "And you are to be helping with the process."

I lift an eyebrow at that. "What? You are supposed to be the one making them."

She folds her arms and scoffs as if she is the captain here. "You have no idea about making doughnuts. Do you know that they are sacred and require specific rituals?"

I stare at her, trying to figure out whether she is serious or just messing with me. I have never baked anything. The kitchen crew doesn't need my help. I grew up trained as a warrior, not a chef or baker.

She groans. "Come on. There won't be doughnuts if you don't do a thing and stand here like a statue."

"Fine..." I open the cupboard to search for the ingredients, then grab some flour. There should be eggs in the fridge. I put everything on the table for her. "Now, what do you still need?"

She starts pouring the ingredients together in the mixing bowl. She hands me a few spoons. "Since I can't seem to find the mixer, you will do this. Use the spoons, and stir the contents until they are mixed well together."

"But that's supposed to be your job."

"I said it takes some magic for the doughnuts to be good."

I think she is messing with me and she just wants to embarrass me and will be laughing at me in her head. I clench a fist, but decide to play along. I will use that for my good later.

"Like this?" I start scooping the flour with the other ingredients, mixing them.

"You have to stand on one foot."

"No way. How is the mixing bowl going to know?"

She tilts her head to the side with a serious glare that makes my heart race. "Are you going to do it or not?"

"Why can't you do it yourself?"

She huffs again. "If I could do it on my own, I would have done it without needing your annoying ass here."

I still don't understand. But I like how she hates to say that she needs me. I stand on one foot and keep stirring the mixing bowl. "Like this?"

She lifts her brows at me. "Yes, you're doing pretty well."

While I have strong arms, mixing this is tiring. Standing on a leg is even dumber.

She clicks her tongue. "Well, are you annoyed or something? That won't make for good doughnuts."

"What?" I stare at her when she rolls her eyes.

"Keep stirring, and do it with a smile. Come on!"

She is annoying me, but at the same time, what if she isn't lying?

"But when you were in the cafe, you were the one making those on your own. You should be able to do that here too."

"It's different. I had special equipment for the doughnuts. You wouldn't understand. Just do as you're supposed to, okay?"

Fine... It's all for doughnuts.

I squeeze out a smile at the mixing bowl, staring at the dough that seems to be slowly getting into shape.

She is at the stove, heating up something. I turn around to glance at her when she catches me at once with a snarl. "Focus, Vrek."

She is lucky at how much I want doughnuts.

It takes a while. Right before I hate this dough enough, Serena is back and she pats my arm. "Okay, you can stop now."

I put the bowl back on the kitchen island. "What's next?"

"Wait."

Oh, did I do something wrong?

She continues, "I mean, we are going to wait."

"What?" I hiss at her. "Why do we have to wait? Don't you put it into the oven and be done with that?"

"No, bigass, that's not how it's done. We aren't making bread."

"What did you just call me?"

"Bigass, what now? Happy vibes create nice dough-nuts."

There's no way this is true.

She moves on to moving the bowl into the oven. I thought we were supposed to make them into the shape of doughnuts before baking them. She checks the setting of the oven, then she comes over to me. "Now, we should..."

I snatch her cheeks into my hands. "Now, the mixing bowl can't hear you. How dare you make me act dumb?"

"Did you call that acting dumb? Geez... You should get out of here before you spoil everything!"

"Now, you are telling me to leave? As if you get to decide—"

She pushes against me, but she is a tiny human and doesn't end up moving me a single inch. I hiss at her, but she doesn't stop. She pushes my chest with the cutest face ever. I like how miserable she is.

I ask, "What are you doing?" I spread my arms to the side, watching her small body still trying.

"I said you should get out of here." She stops and looks up at me; she probably would have stood on her tip toes if she stood a chance at pretending to be taller than me.

"What if I don't want to?"

"Then you'll witness the scary sacrifices for the doughnuts."

"Huh?" My eyes widen at that. "What's the sacrifice?"

She sighs. "Please, you won't want to know. Get out of here. I don't want anything to cause you harm."

Now I'm even more confused than before. It's just doughnuts. She talks as if we're going to tame a monster or something.

She pats my chest again. "Please, just leave. I'll let you know when the doughnuts are ready, but you must not look through the window and you must stay outside."

Um... it feels even more like she's just messing with me and none of it is real, and she's making stuff up. She's probably enjoying my confusion and thinking that she's one-upping me.

But at the same time, what if she isn't lying? Would I be risking all the doughnuts? It should be fine if I stay right outside. She can't get out of the spaceship by staying in the kitchen.

"Okay, I'll leave you alone. But if you dare to stir up anything, I won't hesitate to—"

"Hey, do you still remember our agreement?"

Well... That I won't threaten her again and will treat her as my equal. "That will only be in effect until I have my doughnuts and they taste as good as the ones I had before."

She blinks. "Then you are going to pretend to hate it just so you can keep throwing a fist."

That's not my intention. All I want are nice doughnuts and I don't want her to mess with my food. "No, I'm fair. If it is good, I will say it as is. Be good."

I'm about to pat her head, but her eyes shoot fire at me. Maybe I should think about my balls. But I'm aware of that now, so the chance of her pulling that again and succeeding is low.

I pat her shoulder instead. "You are smart enough to know what to do."

Outside the kitchen, I shiver in the colder corridor. Maybe the kitchen has been too warm and comfortable that it comes at a stark difference.

I lean onto the wall to the side of the kitchen door, tapping my fingers on my arm. Now, Serena is alone in the kitchen with what she called doughnut magic.

No one is walking around in the corridor. This isn't time for the shift changes, so it's going to be quiet for another while. My shift will be coming next, so...

I can only hope she will have the doughnuts ready before my shift starts.

I stare at the kitchen door again. What is she doing inside?

She said I shouldn't look, but the moment she told me what to do, I wanted to ignore all of that.

Doughnuts.

Maybe I shouldn't care that much about those. She is using them to threaten me.

But they are so soft and sweet. I want my doughnuts. And...

Even knowing there's a high chance she's messing with me, I think I enjoy that. Even though she likes to be a brat, she makes me happy.

I want to grab her in my arms and nibble on that soft body. Maybe she will taste even better than doughnuts. I lift my arms in front of me, imagining hugging her.

Maybe when I had her on my lap, I should have tried for something more. But maybe I should wait for a bit longer until she gets comfortable around me.

Comfortable... Is that how she's supposed to feel?

The burn in my stomach is here again, growing stronger and stronger. The heat is spreading along the markings on my body. This is weird.

I suck in a breath, but that doesn't stop the heat. Maybe I'm too focused on her.

Are my doughnuts ready now? Already?

Chapter 10

Serena

I watch the doughnuts sit on the tray, all ready for consumption. Somehow, there's a load in my chest. Vrek finally made me comply and make him doughnuts. Is this a defeat on my part?

I glance at the door. He is probably somewhere outside. He doesn't seem to be looking at me through the window, so maybe my warning worked.

Part of me feels bad for him when he was so innocent and so unsuspecting. But another part of me doesn't mind messing with him. He looked really dumb for doing what I told him to. I managed myself so well that I didn't burst into laughter.

Is he still waiting outside?

It's probably time for me to tell him the doughnuts are ready, but at the same time, that would mean my time alone will come to an end.

He still annoys me.

The glazed doughnuts sit there, quietly watching me. They smell amazing, just like how I used to make them in the cafe.

Pain surges in my stomach and the load in my chest grows. I... That's my life that he took from me and I can never have it back.

But I don't want this. I don't want to be here. These beings think that they can make me do whatever they want, and not care about my decisions.

I clench a fist, but relax it soon enough. There's nothing I can do when the spaceship is still flying. Maybe it will work out if I control myself and pretend to comply.

The spaceship can't keep flying all the time; it has to land somewhere to refuel. These beings have to restock their resources. There will be a chance for me to get out of here.

But I may still never get back to the life I built for myself...

I sniff, fighting to stop the tears from escaping me. I hate every bit of this...

It takes a bit, but when it feels like I can hold it together, I head to the door, opening it before I can regret it. "Vrek?"

He is standing right next to the door as if I would have fled if he wasn't there. He straightens and peeks behind me at the kitchen. "They are ready, right? Smells amazing."

He heads over to the kitchen and doesn't even look at me.

I knew this was how it would go. He's using me. He won't do a single thing we agreed to beforehand. I should know these beings are like that — robbers and kidnappers.

"These are different." He watches the tray of dough-nuts with a confused look. Then he finally remembers my existence. "Serena... Are you crying?"

Am I?

I shake my head. "No, I'm not."

He scowls and comes over to me. "Is everything al-right?"

No, nothing is fine. "You wanted doughnuts and you have them now."

He turns to the tray again. "Are you upset about that?"

"Maybe you should just eat those and be happy about that." I don't want to talk to him.

I keep reminding myself that I'm doing this so I will stand a better chance of fleeing in the future. I should put up a smile and maybe make him happy for that.

But I can't put on a smile and pretend I'm happy. It is a bit too much. I should be good at putting up a face that's good for the circumstances. I've been working at the cafe for long enough and have faced enough beings through all the situations. It shouldn't be hard for me to push it and also look appropriate in front of him.

I take a breath. "Are you going to eat the doughnuts? Or should I tell the others—"

He covers my mouth, looking out into the corridor. "Hush. Come in. I'll close the door."

"You want all the doughnuts for yourself."

He pulls me into the kitchen and slams on the button for the door to close. After the door slides closed, he peeks out of the window. "Geez, if they smell something, they will arrive in no time."

I lean on the wall, not wanting to give a response. I hate this.

He goes to the tray and picks up a doughnut. "Like I just said, this looks different from the ones from last time."

Yeah... His ass doesn't know a thing about doughnuts, and there are more than one type. But I don't want to explain that. I want to be alone.

He takes a bite and his eyes snap open. "Fuck! This is so good."

I turn away from him. I don't even want to see that face.

He is still eating and he seems happy about that. Of course, he would be.

I clench a fist, holding it so tightly that my nails dig into my palm. The lingering pain reminds me of why I'm doing what I did, but...

I almost jump when he shows up right in front of me out of nowhere. He frowns and he holds my cheeks in his ugly big hands.

"Serena... Are you upset? Because I made you make the doughnuts?"

He turns my face to him and he leans over to look me in the eyes, but I still look away, refusing to do as he wishes.

He grunts and he wraps his arms around me. I kick and push, but he won't let go of me. With my height and how he grabbed me, I can't even kick his balls. Maybe he prepared this time around.

"Thank you for the doughnuts."

Yeah... Of course, he would say that. He wants to keep me working for him.

"Serena..."

"You know I hate this."

"I... Maybe our way is very different from humans."

"Is that even between humans and your kind? It should be common knowledge that no being likes to be taken to somewhere they don't want to and to be forced into doing stuff."

He sucks in a deep breath. "I... Well, we're already here now."

I grab his hand, yanking it off my cheek. "Shut up and eat your doughnuts. You already got what you wanted, happy?"

He frowns and doesn't move over to the doughnuts. He's about to say something when the door of the kitchen slides open.

Vrek moves away from me.

In comes a few others that are like Vrek. They squeal and hurry to the tray. "Oh, there are doughnuts!"

Vrek runs over, hurrying to grab a few more.

I suppose there is fun in watching these hulky guys rush and fight with each other for doughnuts. This is probably the craziest thing I've ever seen, other than Vrek kidnapping me just for doughnuts.

There are low growls, punches, and a ton of mess.

Are they that crazy?

But given how their bread sucks, maybe they are dying for decent food. My doughnuts are more than decent.

When the growls and hisses cease, a few of them turn to me. I take a step back at the wall. Are they mad at me?

The tray is empty. They didn't even leave a crumb.

"So, you are the one who made these." One of them comes even closer, giving me a nod. There are still traces of icing on the corner of his lips. He licks the icing with a grin, seemingly in a good mood.

Vrek growls and shoves that guy to the side. "You're scaring her!"

"Hey! You're just crazy. How am I scaring her when I'm just asking?" he growls back at Vrek.

Another to the side steps in between them. "Stop it. Both of you are scaring her."

Vrek and the other guy glare at each other for another moment before they finally take steps backward and the fight is over.

The one who tried to talk to me turns to me again. "The doughnuts are so amazing! We're so happy you're here."

The guy who stood in the middle agrees. "Yes, this is the best thing I've ever had. Will you make us more? I hope you will."

Vrek is sneering at these, barely holding back a growl. All he cares about is keeping all the doughnuts for himself. Maybe I should annoy him.

I nod. "Yes, I'm glad you like them. Once I have lunch, I'll be ready to keep going. I had breakfast a bit too early."

The two squeal and the two others standing next to the kitchen island, a bit further away from me, also grin. Vrek looks worse than when I kicked his balls.

The other big guy reaches his hand out to me, probably trying to shake mine. "Is this humans how greet each other? I'm Riemo."

He's a lot nicer than Vrek, at least on the surface.

"I'm Serena."

I shake his hand. He gives me a forceful shake. Maybe he doesn't realize how much stronger he is compared to me.

Vrek hisses again. "If you hurt that hand, there won't be any doughnuts."

With how mad he is, it feels like there's something more than doughnuts that's bothering him.

Riemo rolls his eyes. "Fine, I'm not going to hurt her. I want doughnuts too. But we have a big fleet, so..."

I ask, "How many are there?"

"There are a hundred of us here. Kind of big compared to a lot of merchant groups."

Oops... That's a lot more than I expected.

Riemo says, "Don't worry, we have patience."

Maybe he has patience, but Vrek sure has none.

Vrek pushes his way in front of me, blocking me off the other male's gazes. "It's okay, she knows what to do. She will walk around and get to know the ship now."

Riemo shrugs. "Fine, it's time for us to prepare lunch for everyone anyway. It's no small feat to keep everyone fed." He winks, seemingly the best among the ones I've met on the ship.

Maybe these are the chefs, and therefore they arrived to get ready for their shift.

Vrek nudges for me to leave. I give the chefs a nod. "Look forward to meeting you again."

They all wave me goodbye and seem to be very happy.

When the door of the kitchen closes and we are out in the corridor, Vrek sneers at the door, then at me. "You were a bit too friendly with them."

"I can't help it, they were nice to me. Maybe that's part of your tactics, but they are nicer."

"I can be nice too!"

"Growling at me doesn't qualify as being nice at all. Did you see how happy they were with the doughnuts?

And how they were so happy I'm here and they asked nicely for more?"

He hisses. "I said I can be nice if that's what you want. You just hate me because I brought you here."

"Obviously, smartass. You have a long way to go."

He leans closer, as if he is showing off his horns at me. "I can be nice."

"I don't see that."

He glares at me for another moment while I contemplate whether I should take a step back. What is he doing with his horns right in front of me, as if he wants to stab me with them?

He grunts and grabs my hand, putting it on the smooth part of his horns. "Here."

Am I supposed to stroke his horns?

Well, if he decides to get mad about that, he did it to himself. I stroke his horn and he lets out a soft groan.

"You're the one who put my hand on your horn."

"Yeah..." He moves away. "Now, we get going."

Maybe that's the way his kind shows kindness. He could have explained more.

I ask, "Where are we going?"

"Walk around, to show you around."

I suppose that's not a bad thing, since I want to flee from the ship in the future. Maybe the chef crew is nicer to me, but it doesn't mean I want to stay here with all these beings. I have my own life, dammit.

"Sure, what do you have on this spaceship? A farm?"

He snorts a laugh. "Don't be dumb. This is a battleship."

Nice, this means they will have to land at some time. I know there are species that have huge spaceships, so huge that generations and generations live there, making it almost a moving planet on its own. If I were kidnapped into one of those, that would probably have been the end of me.

"Then what do you have? A big storage area?"

"Training stadium, lobby for meals, command center, barracks, and that's pretty much it."

"Sounds boring."

He huffs. "What do you mean? Our days are packed."

"Doing what? Mopping the floor? Cleaning the toilets?"

He groans. "Yes and no. How about you stop asking stupid questions?"

"You still have no idea what it means to be nice."

He holds my hand with his huge one. I close my eyes, expecting him to squeeze it so hard that it will hurt.

But he does nothing but hold my hand.

"I'm trying."

Maybe it isn't natural for him to be nice to others. I don't mind feeling his warm hand. His hand is rough, probably from years of battle training. His warmth seems to be seeping into me, heating me from the inside. It's the same weird closeness that I shouldn't feel. What's wrong with him? Or me? Both?

We arrive at a wider corridor, and there is a room down the path which has an opened door. He points ahead. "There, you'll like it."

Um... I don't have the best feeling about that.

Chapter 11

Vrek

I hold Serena's small and soft hand in mine. I like this. We're walking down the corridor to the food lobby, which is probably my favorite place. Who doesn't like food?

She annoys me. Those others were so crazy for her and she... How dare she smile at them as if they made her happy? She should know that she's mine.

Well, I've never told her that. Maybe she has no idea.

Maybe she isn't that happy with the chefs either. She might still be messing with me.

I lick my lips, still enjoying the remaining sweetness of the doughnut in my mouth. It would be a lot better if they didn't come in and ruin everything. I could have had every doughnut to myself. I may not be able to finish all of them, but I still want all of them. She made them and...

"Hey, I thought we were going inside, or at least stopping to check it out." She squeezes my hand, and my cock twitches as if she is stroking me. Something is going wrong with me. I'm not a crazy being like that.

I halt, only to find I almost led her down the corridor a bit too far. I turn around. "Yeah, I was thinking about something."

She lifts her brows, asking without actually asking.

I say, "You make amazing doughnuts."

She remains quiet, peeking into the food lobby instead of looking at me.

I grit my teeth, resisting the urge to hold her cheek and guide her eyes to me. "Everyone's going to like you."

"Yeah, and they will be a lot nicer to me than you."

I silently sigh. Maybe I should be nicer. I don't think I'm that mean. But maybe, like she said, it will take time for her to stop hating me as much.

If she would let me do whatever to her, I would make her happy. The heat inside me always shouts for me to show her what I can do, but I know better than to blindly act on my urges.

I nudge her to go into the lobby with me. There are a lot of tables for everyone. I gesture around. "Most of us are on shift, so we take turns to have food." I take a step to the side, not blocking the door.

Not a lot are there, as some are taking a break and probably decided that staying here is a bit better than staying in their rooms. A few are chatting, but no one is sitting close to the door and I can only hope no one is looking at us. I want to be the only one with her, though I know that's pretty much impossible for now. She is the only human on the ship, so it will be impossible. Everyone will at least be curious.

I continue, "Here, most of us eat at a fixed time together."

She looks around. "So, if I hold a plate of doughnuts here..."

I cover her mouth at once. "No way, I won't let that happen. These animals will eat you alive."

She rolls her eyes. "I said, doughnuts. Come on. You make it sound like I'm standing there naked."

I suck in a deep breath and my hardness hurts me. "Geez... Must you?"

She chuckles. "Looks like you are tempted so hard."

She might have gotten me. I hate that, but she's right. I lean closer to her and she strokes my horn. I shiver from the closeness. I want to be nice to her if that means she will like me more. I want her. Maybe that was another reason it felt like I had to take her here with me, even though I knew she probably didn't want to be here.

"Yes, your existence tempts me. You smell even better than doughnuts."

She glances at the others in the lobby with a naughty smirk. "No wonder you tried to put me on your lap."

"Well, I can't deny that." I lift her chin. "Trust me. I just want you to be here with me. I don't know how to let you understand that I don't mean you harm"

She lifts her brow at me. Before she speaks, I can guess what she wants to say. I spread my arms to the side. "Fine, I'm sorry I kidnapped you. I understand you hate that. I just want you to be happy here too."

She watches me for another moment before she turns away. "So that's the counter where everyone will line up to get their food?"

Maybe she doesn't want to talk about that. I glance at where she is pointing at. "Yes."

It is pretty obvious, since there are a few beings waiting for their food and ones putting food on the trays.

She asks, "What are they eating?"

"We can go and take a look if you want."

"Sure." She starts walking at once. Maybe all she wants is to stay away from me.

Maybe that means she isn't accepting my apologies. I've never apologized to anyone before. There has been no need to do that. But... if that will make her happy. Maybe she would rather have stayed in her cafe.

We arrive at the counter. The one working behind the counter gives us a nod. "Hello there, what do you want?"

She blinks. "What do you have?"

"You can pick between kepolis or nezenta."

She stares at the male, not saying anything. Maybe she has no idea what those are. I say, "Both of us will take nezenta."

"Absolutely." The male turns to fetch our food. Serena glares at me. I shrug. She will understand. I think she will enjoy it over kepolis.

She hisses as she asks, "What's that?"

I tap the tip of her nose. "You will know when you see it."

She huffs. "Pretending to be mysterious? I better actually like it, otherwise..."

I like her.

The male has our food ready and I pick up the tray with our plates and water for both of us. "Enjoy!"

Serena stands on her tiptoe to look at the plate while I lift it all the way up, not letting her peek.

She rolls her eyes at me. "You love to mess around with me."

"As if you don't like to mess with me?"

We arrive at a table and I set the tray down. She looks at it. "So... Nezenta is spaghetti and meat."

"Yes, and kepolis is the bread roll that you seemed to hate."

She blinks. "I still have to decide whether I like this or not."

We take a seat. She is barely tall enough for the table to work for her. Her legs are probably dangling. She peeks under the table; maybe she doesn't like to be short.

She turns to me and glares at me. "Are you laughing at me?"

"No, I'm not."

"Your smirk outs you."

Am I smirking? I shrug. "Are you tall enough for the big boys' table?"

"Looks like you're waiting to have your balls kicked."

I swallow. No one wants that. She looks like the one who can and will remember that to the end of the world. If I wrong her, she is going to find a chance to kick me, and it's going to hurt.

I clear my throat. "Maybe you should try the food."

She picks up the fork and scoops up the spaghetti with the sauce. The food smells amazing and I hope she will like it. She eats the whole forkful and blinks. My breath hitches for a moment.

"It's not that bad. At least the sauce is good." She stabs up a slice of the roasted meat with the fork and chews it. "I think I like the meat too. Maybe your chefs are just bad at baking."

The bread roll wasn't that bad... And the toast I gave her also couldn't be that bad. Maybe humans have very different tastes from me.

She keeps eating, so it probably means she likes the food.

I pick up my fork and start eating too. I wasn't hungry, but as soon as I saw and smelled food, I couldn't stop myself. The sauce is my favorite and the meat here is always great.

She focuses on the food, seemingly hungry too. Making doughnuts probably tired her out.

I eat my food, but something seems to inch close to my plate from her side. I look, but before I can do a thing, she forks a slice of my meat. I growl at her.

She ignores me and puts the meat into her mouth. She eats it and smiles so widely that... While I've been eating the meat too, she makes that slice look a lot tastier than the rest of the slices.

She blinks. "I think this is the best slice."

I huff. "As if I'm going to believe you."

"You don't have to." She licks her fork for the last drop of sauce. The way she licks the fork... She makes my cock twitch. She could lick my cock and I could...

"Vrek?"

I blink and yank my gaze back to her. "Yes?"

Her eyes narrow on me. "What are you thinking about?"

"Nothing."

Her gaze grows stronger and seems to be staring through me. I swallow and she leans closer. "Are you going to lie to me?"

"I mean it."

"I don't believe you."

I look away when something pats my thigh. I spin around and stare at her. "What are you doing?"

She strokes my thigh and her hand reaches closer and closer to my cock. "But it seems like you're thinking about a lot of things."

I suck in a breath. "Are you sure about that? Don't ask if you don't want to hear the answer."

She moves even closer. "What's on your mind? Wanting some action? After you ate the doughnuts, you want something more?"

"Well, this is your answer. If there weren't all the others here, I'd pin you on the table and take you already."

"Are you scared? Do you think they will also want a slice?"

"No one gets to take a slice or a bit, or even put a finger on you."

She lifts her brows at me. "You're so serious about that."

I suck in a breath. "I am." I cup her cheeks in my hands. "I mean it."

She blinks, seemingly understanding something even though I didn't mean to say it like that.

Her eyes narrow on me and it feels like I'm naked. I continue, "Like I said, I want you. I want the doughnuts, but you are more important than that."

"What do you mean?"

I want to kiss her and figure out what those lips taste like, but... There are others here and I'm not supposed to like Serena. It's already a stretch to have a female here on the spaceship. If I kiss her...

Well... I'm holding her cheek already, and that doesn't seem like I'm threatening her. Before I waste even more time thinking about that, I peck a kiss on the tip of her nose.

I let go of her, staring at my plate again. Maybe she doesn't want that and is afraid to let me know, though she doesn't seem like someone who will be intimidated.

I hate how it feels like I can't do a single thing to bring us closer. Maybe I shouldn't have kidnapped her. If I asked, would she have agreed to come onto the spaceship with me?

She remains at her place, watching me for another moment before she picks up her fork again. She eats without giving a word or any reaction to the kiss.

I would have kissed her lips, but I don't want her to hate me for that. What if she doesn't want that?

I glance at her, but she seems to be focused on her food, which I don't believe is the case.

Maybe that wasn't a good idea after all... Maybe I can never do the right thing.

Chapter 12

Serena

My heart is still racing even after we leave the cafeteria.

What did Vrek just say, even though I heard him clearly?

He is walking ahead of me with his hands on his waist. Maybe he doesn't want to hold my hand anymore.

I tilt my head to the side, watching his back. My eyes travel along the markings on his body. Do they mean something?

He keeps walking, maybe also deep in thoughts. I don't understand him. It wouldn't be bad if he treated me nicer, but at the same time, it feels like he's trying to say something more important than that. What else does he want from me other than doughnuts?

Maybe he wants to fuck me, like he mentioned. I... Maybe his strong arms can hug me well and that muscular body is good for cuddling.

He turns around, and I almost bump into him. "Serena, I mean it. I want more than just doughnuts."

He looks around, seemingly trying to make sure we're alone. "I know I'm not that good at acting nice, but..."

I shrug. "You confuse me. You started off trying to kill me, but now, you seem to be jealous when the other guys like me."

"No one gets to like you."

"Why?" I fold my arms and stare at him. "I'm not owned by anyone. And they can like me however they want."

He grunts. "You see, I brought you to the ship, so you're mine."

I roll my eyes at that, but my heart is beating stronger. "No way. That's not how it works. I'm not owned by anyone. I'm not an object you can own because you picked it off the floor. I'm a fucking human. You can't just kidnap me and think that I'm yours."

"That's not how it works with me."

"You don't get to own me."

"I do. You are here to stay."

"So much for saying you can be nice."

"I'm just honest. You aren't leaving here anytime soon, not a chance."

I grit my teeth. I hate him. "Maybe you can lock me up here, but I'll never like you."

He remains quiet, blinking as if he's never thought about that before.

I shrug. "You know that's what it is. You can kidnap beings, but you can't control how they feel and think."

He sighs. "I don't mean to hurt you. It's just..."

I look away from him. "I never imagined that being good at baking would get me into trouble."

He rests his hands on my shoulders. "I... I'm sorry."

I don't think he is as sorry as he said he is.

He remains quiet, watching me as if he wants a response from me.

Silence lingers between us, which I don't like. But instead of saying the wrong thing or giving him the wrong impression, I'd rather say nothing.

He keeps watching me. This is probably the most patience he has ever shown. Does that mean he really cares? And he will wait until I say something?

His breath turns ragged, like he is fighting to stop fidgeting from boredom. He swallows and it feels like every hair on him is standing up. Is he going to grab my throat and make me say something?

He rubs his horns, then puts his hands on his waist. But it doesn't take a long time before he puts them to his sides instead, then on his hips.

"Vrek."

"Yes."

"Tell me, what do you want with me?"

"For you to make doughnuts and warm my bed."

I lift an eyebrow at that. He has to be hiding something from me. Maybe it isn't time for him to say it. I wonder what that could be.

He reaches for my hand, squeezing it. "Here, I'll show you the training field. I think some others may be there, but we can peek from the balcony."

So... Did he stop waiting for my response to his apology? Or did he take my question as an acceptance?

"Vrek, I'm not done. I won't forget about everything this quickly. I'm still going to hate this place and nothing will change. You didn't even keep up your end of the bargain."

"I know. I still have a long way to go to prove myself to you, right?"

Yes, and it seems like he finally understands that. "I'll give you a chance."

He halts and I almost bump into him again. At least all he has are horns, not spikes on the back, otherwise, I'm going to be dead someday.

He asks, "Are you sure? Did I hear that right? Are you going to give me a chance?"

Now, and I wonder whether I should regret that. But if he likes me more, maybe it will make it easier for me to flee in the future. "Yes, but you'll have to prove yourself."

He grins so widely that my stomach sinks. It feels bad to lie to him. I stare at him for another moment, but before I'm done thinking about that, he starts walking again. "Here, I'll show you everything."

He is so happy...

The heat that has been lingering in me grows again. How bad will it be if I stay with him?

I close my eyes, trying to stop myself from thinking about that. I'm supposed to be fighting to go back to my own life. But in my mind, all I can see is how he can pin me on a wall and hug me so tightly that I may choke, but in a good way. And... He will be so happy when we get to share doughnuts.

When I open my eyes again, we are already walking. He is a step in front of me, oblivious to my thoughts. He is different from other guys I've been with. I've never run into someone who is crazy enough to kidnap me like this.

"Here." He stops and points at a door. I glance at the inside. It is dim and doesn't look like anyone is there. He gently squeezes my hand and nudges me to go in with him.

We are in the darkness for a few steps before lights come on from downstairs. We are on a balcony with seats to the sides, but maybe there's nothing to watch, as the lights are off.

There are occasional shouts and the clanking sound of knives or something hard hitting each other. Probably weapons, not knives.

We arrive at a dwarf wall. There are beings down there fighting, practicing their warrior ways. I shiver at how they look like they are trying to kill each other. They are huge beings compared to me, making those weapon swings and growls even stronger. They are smacking against each other's weapons, but it feels like they are hammering on me instead.

Vrek wraps an arm around me, pulling me to his side. "Don't worry, they won't hurt you. I won't let them hurt you. More importantly, these weapons are for training use, so no one will get injured."

"Like... badly injured?"

"Well, if you trip and fall, some can be injured. But the healing appliances are going to fix most of the injuries."

"That doesn't sound too interesting." I shudder at that. I eye Vrek up and down. There aren't any injury marks on him. "Have you gotten injured in training before?"

He rolls his eyes. "No, don't worry about that. The chance of that is very low. We know it's just a training session and none of us are out there to kill each other."

I turn to the field downstairs again. In the rectangular battlefield, beings are... trying to kill each other. But maybe for them, that's just play or practice. "How about in actual fights? You said you guys are warriors."

He frowns. "Yeah, we do attack villages and places. No wonder some call us robbers or the bandits."

I suck in a breath as my back seems to tense up. "You said you do what?"

He smirks and pats my head. I should kick his balls like I did, but my body is so tight that I can't move. "Serena, you are cute. We are warriors, and we attack spaceships and villages."

I point at him, but I can't make out a single word. I don't want to be making doughnuts and staying with monsters like these.

He continues when I don't say anything. "You see, I won't hurt you. We won't hurt you."

"That's not the point. How can you do that?"

He shrugs. "Just making a living."

"How can you do that? It's just evil to attack innocent beings."

"Don't care. It's always been like that anyway. Beings attacking each other. Maybe you're a bit too blessed to live in a city and don't have to fight for your life."

I stare at him, not believing what I heard. "And you want me to help you when all you do is hurt others."

He lifts my chin and strokes my cheek. "We are just different. Sometimes, we fight other bandits, and some-times, we rob the Empire's spaceships. We only take the stuff and we spare the beings if they don't fight us."

"That doesn't make it any better." I fold my arms and look away from him. "I can't do this. I don't want to be on this ship."

"Hey!" He wraps his arms around me and pulls me over to him, despite the fact that I want to leave and I want to be alone. I have to at least process everything. I thought they were merchants, but apparently...

I shiver when my back presses against his strong chest. He gives me the annoying heat between my legs again. But I don't want that.

He lets out a soft groan. "Please, I just want to be honest with you."

"Shut up."

He covers my mouth. "Hush, we aren't supposed to be here."

What's even in his mind? A moment ago, he said he would be nice to me and...

But maybe what his fleet does for a living isn't part of that and has nothing to do with whether he is nice or not. But I don't understand.

He strokes my side. "Listen, I know this isn't a life you've ever imagined or agreed with, but trust me, we aren't pure evil. On your planet, it is peaceful, but that's not the case everywhere. We fight when we have to, but—"

"You said you attack ships and villages."

"Yes, at times."

"You could have done something better and something without violence."

"We were born to fight."

"You can choose not to."

"Part of me wishes I could. But we aren't even the bad ones around here. At times, we rehome beings."

"Rehome? You fucking kidnapped me! Is that what you call rehoming?"

"I didn't sell you and won't hurt you. You know there are worse beings out there."

I close my eyes. "Stop it... I know I can't get out of here, but please..."

"Would you rather I lie to you? When you will eventually find out?"

"I... I don't like this at all."

"I wish I had something nicer to tell you, but it is what it is."

A load forms in my chest again. I thought we could at least be less hostile toward each other for a moment, but I don't know what I should do or say now. I don't like that, but maybe he has a point or two that I don't understand.

He sighs. "Do you want to go back to the room?"

I nod with my eyes still on the ground. Maybe that'll be for the best. I need some time on my own.

Chapter 13

Vrek

"Vrek, what are you doing?" the coach growls at me.

I flinch, lowering my weapon when it feels like my head has been somewhere else. "Coach..."

He comes over and yanks the battle axe out of my hand. "What are you doing? We are practicing for fights. I know no one is going to die, but can you at least try harder?"

I have been trying hard. There's no reason for the coach to...

I bite my tongue to stop myself from talking back. It isn't like the coach would mention that if he could see my effort in the training. "I'm sorry."

"Let's keep going."

My training companion, Zil, frowns at me, but he lifts his weapon and aims it at me. I do the same and we resume our practice, not wanting to be the spot of attention anymore.

I dodge his slash, slamming my axe at him. He blocks, the recoil shaking my axe. He leans closer. "Hey, are you sick?"

I shake my head. Both of us take a step back before we run into each other again, practicing what we are told to do for this shift. "I'm fine."

The others are also around, the sounds of weapons clashing against each other and a few grunts here and there make our chat less obvious.

"Are you sure?"

I grit my teeth when he hits me hard, gathering strength to push back at him. Zil is a strong male too, a respectable fighter.

"Yes, I'm more than certain about that."

We keep going. I like the motion. Maybe it will keep my mind off Serena. I left her in my room, telling her to stay there and wait for me so no one will be too curious about her. I want to be there with her longer, all the time, but I have a duty to fulfill.

She hates how the fleet survives. I think I understand, but maybe... Is that a deal breaker for her? She probably thinks we are evil. All we're trying to do is to stay alive. The world is a dangerous place. If you don't have the ability to fight, you'll be eaten alive.

I take a breath as even more heat pools in me. Maybe it's from the combat training, or maybe it's from how much I miss her.

Zil hisses and I blink. I barely dodge his slash. Training battle axes aren't sharp and at worst, I'd get an ugly bruise all over my face and be the laughingstock for a while, but I want neither.

I shake it off and scowl at myself. I better try harder. There will be time to think about Serena later.

When the training session is finally over, I'm covered with sweat from head to toe. Zil isn't looking any better. We return the training weapons and turn to leave together.

The others are also leaving. There are chatters in the air. What is Serena doing?

"Hey, are you sure you aren't sick or something?" Zil asks again.

"I'm fine. What's wrong with you?" We are on good terms, and that includes teasing each other at times.

He shrugs. "I don't know. Your mind seemed to be elsewhere the whole time. Is that about the female?"

"No, nothing's special about her. I think I'll get her working soon enough."

Zil folds his arms. "I wonder how the doughnuts tasted. You went out of the way to get the human here."

"Yeah, and you almost killed her."

"Hey, that's not true." He spreads his arms to the side. "I was trying to help, or she would have kicked your balls."

My heart skips a beat. I suppose Serena found her chance since. "I could handle her. I told you to be there just so we wouldn't be spotted."

"Whatever you like to say. She's here now, but I haven't had a single doughnut yet. Don't you think something is wrong about that?"

"There will be doughnuts for everyone." That's if she doesn't refuse to make more now that she knows what the fleet does.

"And you're keeping her? Or did Captain give her her own room?"

"He said nothing."

Zil lifts an eyebrow at me when we are out of the field and into the corridor again. "So, you're keeping her in your room."

My heart races and hammers in my chest. I know I'm not supposed to, but... I didn't ask Captain where to put her, not wanting a chance for him to have other arrangements. "Yes, she's with me."

Zil narrows his eyes on me. "Well, you better be careful."

"Huh? Are humans dangerous?"

She kicked my ass and balls and that hurt, but she wouldn't be able to do that again. I don't think she is that dangerous.

Zil says, "No, but you know why there are no females on the ship, and that's not because Captain wants to annoy us."

"He agreed when I asked whether we could bring her here."

"Yeah... But... I mean, you understand what I'm getting at."

I sigh. "Don't worry, she won't distract me."

Zil muses without saying anything. I don't think he wants to take Serena from me anyway, he isn't that kind of male. But Captain...

We walk down the corridor, arriving at the lift. I press the button and we move to the side, letting the others also come closer to the lift and wait.

The lift is soon filled with sweaty uzains, which isn't pleasant at all. At least it's just a single floor and I can tolerate that.

I let out a breath as we leave the elevator. Zil and I exchange a glance and a smile. Maybe everyone else is thinking the same thing.

Soon, we arrive at the branch of the corridor where the food area and rooms are on different sides. Zil asks, "Are we going to grab food together? Or do you have other plans?"

I glance at the side that leads to my room. I want to be with Serena, but at the same time, it feels like I shouldn't shove Zil to the side as soon as Serena is here.

Zil pats my shoulder. "Maybe you aren't hungry yet, huh?"

I shake my head. "No, I was thinking maybe she is hungry too. I left her in the room and told her not to wander so she wouldn't end up where she shouldn't be. I'll get her and meet you in the food area."

Zil snickers. "Well, I'm not going to wait for you before I start eating then." He looks behind us, where more should be coming down the corridor in no time. "I'll reserve two seats for you if you end up showing up."

I roll my eyes when he is already heading off. So much for thinking I'll be distracted that easily.

It won't take long to get Serena out of the room, given she stayed there.

Chapter 14

Serena

I stare at the door after Vrek left. He said it was his round for training, so he would be there and I had to be here and wait for him to be back.

He sneered and showed off his horns, warning me to stay in the room.

Now... Do I listen to him and stay here?

I pat the bed. It's tempting to take a nap. But at the same time, I want to see what's around here.

But... What if I run into others and they don't know that I'm here? This team is pretty big, and who knows what the others will do if they think I'm an invader? So... I shiver at the thought. Being chased down the corridor by these huge guys won't be fun.

But if I stay here and do nothing, listening to Vrek perfectly, will he think that I've accepted what his fleet did?

I take a breath, trying to calm my heartbeat. But these beings are bandits and they rob others for their own lives. I hate that.

The cold and quiet room seems to be staring at me. This is Vrek's room and it smells like him, as if he is around and watching me.

If I let him hold me in his arms, he will warm me. But at the same time, maybe I shouldn't want him. He is the one who kidnapped me. I can hate him for that and I don't have to feel bad about that.

But when he swore he would be nice to me and seemed to be trying...

The heat in my stomach grows. It feels right when he is around, even though nothing about that is right.

I don't understand.

Why do I think about him? Because he has strong muscles? Because he has handsome horns?

Thinking about him makes me hot.

I shake my head and stand up from the bed. I have to calm my mind. Around the room, there isn't a lot of stuff that's interesting. His room has a bed, a table and chairs, a wardrobe, and that's pretty much everything. On the table, there's nothing, nada. Nothing here shows his liking and this room could be anyone's.

Does he not like anything and doesn't want to keep anything here? Or does he own nothing and therefore have nothing to show for his work here? How can that be?

I know feeding everyone on the fleet isn't cheap at all, but if they keep attacking others, they should have more than enough to support themselves.

Is Vrek hiding something from me? I don't like that they are bandits, but at the same time... Maybe as he said, I would rather him be honest with me, which isn't wrong.

If that's the case, maybe he didn't lie and he tried his best to tell me everything.

I let out a breath and with my legs walking on their own, try to pace enough to take my mind off him. But I'm here in his room and on his spaceship, so how can I not think about that?

There is a button on the wall, out of nowhere. It can't be a button that will destroy the ship anyway.

Vrek told me to stay in the room, but he didn't say I couldn't press buttons. More importantly, I don't have to listen to him if I don't want to. And I have to let him know that he doesn't own me, even though he thinks he does.

Owns me...

He's such a crazy guy. First, he came to my cafe when his fleet probably landed on the planet for refueling and restocking. I don't think it was pure luck. So, he searched and came for the doughnuts. Then he kidnapped me for even more doughnuts.

How much crazier can he be?

Do I want someone who is crazy enough for doughnuts to insist on how he wants me?

The way he cupped my cheek and hinted at how he wants me and how that's more than how he wants doughnuts comes back to my mind again.

His hands are so warm and his body...

I sigh. Maybe I should press the button and check what it is for. It should at least take my mind off him and off how... I'm still confused about how to process the situation.

A door slides open. It's the bathroom. Well, that's not interesting at all. There is a toilet, the shower room, and that's pretty much everything.

I let out a sigh, staring at the clean white walls inside. This is such a boring place. Does he not have any fun? He has pretty much nothing in his room, like... does he even live here?

It must be a stupid boring life with only training, helping to drive the spaceship, fighting, eating, and that's all about it. Maybe he can also chat with others, but that's all.

Ah... Maybe that's why he wants doughnuts that badly. Poor him, not having any fun.

There is a hiss behind me. I almost jump. Through the door comes Vrek. Is his training already over? Just like that? Have I been sitting on the bed doing nothing for so long? Or pacing around for so long?

He grins when he sees me. "You're here."

"Yeah... So?" I fold my arms. I haven't had time to mess around with him yet. "How long was your training session?"

"A few hours."

What the fuck... Time flies here on a stupid spaceship.

He sighs. "You still hate me."

"Yes."

He spreads his hand to the side. "I can't lie to you. That's all we can do to stay alive in an area that hates us."

I look away from him. I know there are bad beings around and for some species, it isn't that easy. But at the same time, I understand to a point. "It's with the Empire, right?"

He nods. "Yes."

Maybe I understand that a bit more. Can't say that's a part of life that I enjoy. I usually try to forget about that and just operate my cafe the best I can. "I'm tired."

"Huh? What did you do?"

"Exist."

"Oh... I hope you aren't upset, like... Not too upset."

I shrug. "As if there's something I can do?"

He sighs again. "Okay, I'm here to ask whether you want to eat with me in the food zone, or for me to bring you food here, or for you to pick your food and bring it here on your own."

I guess this is the first time I can choose something. That's a small one that's not that significant, but it's better than nothing. "I'll go and check out the food."

He nods. "Zil, my training partner, will also be there if you decide to join us. The food zone may be busy since my session just ended and the others are probably also going for food."

"Doesn't bother me. I know this ship is filled to the brim with your kind."

"We are uzains."

"Yeah, that." I turn around. Maybe I should rethink that. The whole ship with uzains... There are probably a dozen or two— No, maybe fifty uzains in the cafeteria, and I will be the only human there. Not to mention, maybe for a lot of them, I'm a slave or something that Vrek brought here to work for them. At least the captain of the ship sure thinks that.

"Vrek."

"Yes."

"What will others think about me? That I'm a slave, someone who they can toss to the side or hurt whenever they want?"

He shakes his head. "No, it's not like that. I won't let anyone hurt you." He turns his head from side to side, showing off his horns. "Look, I can and I will protect you."

"What do the rest of your fleet think? I'm a punching bag?"

"I don't think they will think that. You already met the cooking team and you know they are... Well, not aggressive."

I tilt my head to the side. I suppose he isn't wrong. They were very nice to me. Maybe it was because of the doughnuts.

He comes closer and pats my shoulders. "If you don't want to go there, it's fine. I'll bring you food before meeting my training partner. You can stay here if you want."

Maybe he is trying to treat me nicer. I say, "I can tag along. I hope you have better food than strange bread."

He grins and that warms me. I shouldn't be that impressed by that, but I like that. I like it when he isn't growling and hissing at me.

He squeezes my hand. "Let's go."

I go with him, but when we get out of his room, he lets go of my hand. He says, "I want to hold your hand, but I'm not supposed to feel anything for you. There's a reason there isn't a single female here, regardless of species."

"Females are good at distracting you? Or you are too bad at focusing?"

He grunts. "That's not me. I think that's a very common rule on spaceships like this."

"I don't know about that. I've never been on a bandit ship."

He sighs again. "I said that's not a choice. I'm not you."

"But you are fine with that."

He remains quiet, so I pat his arm. "I understand though. It's just a bit too different and not what I was expecting."

He puts up a smile. "I hope that means something good."

"Maybe."

He lets out a soft groan but with a smirk. Maybe I like him this way too.

At the cafeteria, the moment I walk through the door, I regret it. This place is packed full of uzains. Like, they are everywhere. I know this is their ship and everyone here is a uzain, but there are a lot of them here, not like the last time I was here.

This place is buzzing with them walking around with trays of food, and those already sitting and munching down their food. At the counter, there are quite a lot lining up and waiting for their food. I take a step behind Vrek before I realize it. I'm going to be the only woman here on the spaceship and among all of these beings who are bigger and stronger than me, and that's not very pleasant.

Vrek turns around at me. "Hey, are you fine? You look pale."

I take a breath. My heart hammers in my chest and my head is light. "Um... I'm fine."

"Excuse me," someone behind me talks and I jump. "Whoa! Did I scare you? Sorry." It's a big guy trying to get his food and since I flinched at the door, I'm blocking his path.

Vrek nudges my stiff body to the side. "Sorry about that."

I open my mouth, but I can't get out a word. The big guy watches me with a frown. Vrek shrugs. "All good. She is trying to get used to being here."

The big guy nods. "Maybe I scared her. I didn't mean to."

I murmur. "I know. I..." My voice trails off, though I doubt he can hear a single word when it is noisy in here.

Vrek pats my shoulder and tells the guy, "I suppose being the only one who's different from everyone else is intimidating at times."

The guy says, "I suppose so. Hope you get used to this. We don't mean to hurt you. I'll get in line now, see you." He walks off and finally, it feels better.

Vrek turns to me again. "See? Those of us here aren't mean."

I nod, still not knowing what to say. My body is still tense and my throat is tight.

Vrek looks around and nudges me to go with him. "There, I found Zil."

I follow, fighting my urge to run out of the door already. When I was in the cafe, I met all kinds of beings too. Yet, I never felt like this before. In the city center, there were are a lot of beings who weren't humans too, but none of them made me feel like this.

While it isn't these uzains' fault for how I feel, it is just... a bit too much for me all at once.

We are heading to someone who looks as strong as Vrek. They almost look the same, except this one is sitting and busy with his food. Their horns are different, but otherwise, they look kind of the same. Coal-gray, longer black hair with laser-intense eyes.

"Zil." Vrek pats the guy's back, so hard that he shudders and the food on his spoon drops back onto the plate.

Zil grunts. "Vrek... Oh, and human. Hi. What's your name?"

"Serena." At least I can still say my own name. Now that we are at a table, I try to focus on Zil instead of all the others around us. Maybe that will help.

Zil also frowns at me. "Are you fine? Are you sick? Hungry?" He turns to Vrek. "What have you done to her? She's so pale."

Vrek grunts. "Exist? I don't know why she's pale. Maybe your existence scares her."

Zil chuckles. "Are you sure I'm the reason? Maybe she's hungry and you should get her food. The line is long."

Vrek glances at the line and he sighs. "You aren't wrong." He pulls a chair, gesturing for me to take a seat. "I'll get you food. You can wait for me here. Zil doesn't poke, so you don't have to worry. His horns are only there for decoration."

I snort a laugh at that. At least Vrek makes me happier and less tense; he has some use.

Zil rolls his eyes. "Come on, you know I have strong horns. But feel free to sit with me. I won't hurt you. Not that any of us here will. We are still waiting for the doughnuts, but it is totally fine if you want a bit more time to get used to this place and us. There are a lot of us though, so I hope it won't take too long."

I take a breath, sitting on the chair. There is an empty space between Zil and me, around the corner of the table, which is for Vrek.

ZIl gives me a nod. "Feel free to ask questions or talk if you want to." He lowers his head soon enough, continuing with his food.

He is munching on a deep plate of orange things. It looks like curry or a stew, but I'm not sure whether it's going to taste like curry.

It looks like he is enjoying his food. So I hope it is good.

But... The rock-hard toast in the morning still haunts me.

Chapter 15

Vrek

I stand in line, and I can't stop rubbing my horn. I hate how I have to wait here. Why are there so many of us here waiting for food? Maybe whoever is working at the counter should do stuff quicker.

My eyes are glued onto Serena, who is so far away from me. She looks quiet and nervous. I hate to have to leave her behind like that. I know Zil can be trusted, but I still don't like it.

But at the same time, it isn't like Serena will appreciate coming out here to be in the line with me. She won't like to feel like the spot of attention where everyone can be watching her. I don't think everyone's that curious, but she won't like that regardless.

It takes forever until it is finally my turn to order. The one on duty gives me a nod and starts preparing the food, not asking what I'm choosing. So I guess there's no option for dinner. I tell him to give me two servings.

The food smells good and I hope Serena will like it.

I glance in her direction again. She is still sitting there, stiff like a statue. I want to be back with her already.

"Your food is ready."

"Oh, sorry about that." I take the tray and hurry off before the ones behind me complain.

Serena looks toward me. I hope that means she at least misses me a tiny bit. She warms me and makes it hard for me to control myself. I want to growl and squeal, but that's not because I'm mad. I just have to... let out the excitement in me. But that might scare her, and I don't want her to think of me as a monster.

I arrive and set down the tray, giving her a plate and a glass of water. She is safe. Zil didn't hurt her. They aren't talking, but maybe that's because Zil has been busy with his food, which I don't mind.

She glances at the plate. "So... What's this?"

"It is made of spicy sauce and roasted meat. There are also slices of bread inside."

She scowls at once. "Bread, the kind you made the toast with, right?"

"Well, yes."

Zil lifts his head from his plate. "What's wrong with the bread?"

Serena winces and sighs. "Really? Is that even a question? The bread is rock-hard."

Ah, rock-hard. She is the one who often makes me rock hard. My cock, which I want to taste her with. But that's not something I should be thinking about for now.

I shrug. "With the sauce, it can't be that bad. Have a try. At least you can have some meat. You seemed to like it for lunch."

She picks up the spoon regardless and starts eating. Maybe she doesn't hate the food.

I start with my food when something climbs onto my thigh. There can't be bugs or animals here, right?

Serena is looking at me. Maybe that's her hand. I reach for my thigh and find her soft hand there. It's cold and it feels lifeless. She looks at her food now, scooping up the shreds of bread alongside the meat. I put food into my mouth too, just so we won't look too awkward.

Zil apparently isn't looking at us, but I think he knows, or he can guess what's happening.

He keeps eating, not saying much.

Serena also keeps eating, so maybe she is nervous and not sure what to say.

I swallow the meat, looking around to make sure no one seems to be aggressive with Serena. I won't let anyone hurt her. Even though she hasn't agreed to be mine, I'm going to keep a close eye on that.

Zil clears his throat when he puts the spoon to the side, finally finishing his food. "See, it looks like I'm the one in the way between the two of you."

I shake my head. "Not at all. There's nothing between us. You don't have to worry about that."

He chuckles, and doesn't seem to be convinced. "Ah, that's what you have to say, huh? Don't worry, I won't tell anyone. You just have to control yourself." He stands and picks up his tray. "My friend. Play smart."

I'm about to say something when Serena squeezes my thigh, pulling my attention to her instead. I quickly give Zil a nod goodbye and look at Serena. "What? Something's up?"

She shakes her head, but the frown on her face seems to be saying something else. "I... I don't know. Am I bothering you? Am I going to cause you issues? Like... I'm not supposed to be close to you? Not even like this?"

I grunt. "I don't care. While I'm not Captain, I'll do whatever I can do to make sure you'll do great here."

"Everything for the doughnuts?"

I take in a breath. "No. Well, yes, and no. I want that, but I also want you."

"Greedy."

She sends warmth into my stomach. "I want it all, yes. Like Zil implied, Captain may not like this. But I don't want to care about that. I just want you to be happy even though you aren't here because you want to be."

She remains quiet and keeps eating.

My stomach twitches, but I make myself keep talking. "I really hope... that's possible."

She strokes my thigh. Even though she isn't saying much, I hope she agrees with me.

Chapter 16

Serena

We are finally back in his room, which is far better than being in the cafeteria when I was the only weirdo there. I've been a weirdo before, but when there are a lot of different species in the room, a human is not that obvious.

Vrek stretches his arms, probably wanting to show off his muscles. "I'm full. But at the same time, I'm so tired."

"Yeah, you ate so much."

These beings have big plates and servings, which is a bit too much for me. I gave almost half of my serving to Vrek, who seems to be able to eat more after finishing his portion. I was so stuffed that I couldn't have another bite.

The orange sauce wasn't curry. It was spicy with other types of herbs. It feels like they also cooked and mashed potatoes or similar roots into the sauce, making it thick and extra filling. There were shreds of bread, but as Vrek said, with the sauce, they were a lot better. The meat was great like before. They tasted like chicken, but a bit more gamey, which I liked.

Vrek pats my stomach. "Your tiny body can't take that much, huh?"

I lift my brows at him. Is he hinting at something else?

He clears his throat, probably also realizing that. "Look, what I mean is…"

"You're the naughty one."

"Maybe."

My cheeks are burning, and worse, the tingles between my legs are heating up.

He leans closer to me and I take a step away from him.

He looks… upset and seemingly hurt.

I point at the button for the bathroom. "You should take a shower. I hope you do that all the time."

"Hey, I don't smell that bad, come on." He huffs and grunts, but heads over there.

I laugh at that. He is not as sweaty as when he picked me up for dinner, but I love teasing him.

He presses the button for the bathroom, but he yanks me inside with him. "Here, you have to learn the system."

"Is that an excuse to get me naked or make me look at your naked body?"

He grunts. "Come on. I'm totally innocent. You are the one thinking about that all the time."

"Hey, that's not true. You're the one— Whoa!" I step on something and trip. Before I know it, I'm in his arms.

He grins. "Look at you. Using all your ways to get into my arms, huh?"

I swear he did something. Maybe he was the one who tripped me. "It's not like that! Come on! Let go of me!"

He laughs. "It's okay if you want me."

"And it's okay if you just be honest about the fact that you're just horny."

He turns around and pins me on the wall of the showering area. "Maybe I am. Are you going to do something about that? Or want to do something with me?"

I know this is a bad idea. But somehow, it feels like I want that too. He grins and his strong muscles seem to be throbbing with heat and strength. How bad can that be anyway?

"Vrek, admit it, you need me."

He takes in a breath, puffing his chest and showing off his horns even more. "Maybe."

I stroke his chest. "Maybe? That doesn't sound good enough."

He snorts and rolls his eyes. "Fine, I need you, so take my cock already."

Fuck... My body is burning. There seems to be a hum inside my body, screaming for me to let him hold me and do whatever he wants to me. This makes no sense, but when have things made sense with him?

I pat his chest again. "Cutting to the chase, huh?"

"Yes." His hand goes under my clothes, sneaking up to my bra. His huge and rough hand cups my breast. "Hmm... Soft and nice."

I moan and run my hand down his chest to his belt. "What are you hiding under this?"

"You will know very soon."

"But I want to know now." I fiddle with his belt, trying to get it off him. He already has both of my boobs in his hands. He squeezes and plays with them, sending pleasure through me.

It doesn't take long before all our clothes are gone. He pins me even tighter at the wall, pressing his muscular chest onto my boobs. "You are ready for me."

I gasp when he takes my hand and puts it on his cock. I can't see it, but he has a huge one, matching his muscular body.

His cock isn't a smooth one, maybe... There are thick bands on his cock and it pulses with heat, as if teasing me and challenging me.

He grins even wider. "Are you scared? Do you still want to continue?"

"Geez, you think that you're that scary, huh?"

"Brave?" He shoves his hand between my legs, rubbing my folds. "I like how soft you are, and you're so wet."

"Maybe you should actually do something meaningful instead of pure talk."

He shoves his finger into me and I flinch. He has a thick finger and he starts moving it in and out of me at once. I moan and my pussy squeezes against him, milking for more.

He lifts my chin with his other hand. "Are you wet enough for me?"

"Vrek..." My body is burning and I don't want to care whether fucking him is a good idea anymore. I spread my legs some more. He grabs them and parts them even wider.

"Oh!" I moan when he pushes his tip into me. He is thick and he stretches me so hard that I might break.

He stops and takes a breath. "So tight. So much better than my imagination."

"You've been wanting this."

"Oh, yes. I didn't when all I wanted was to get you here so you could make me doughnuts, but after you got here, I can't stop myself. Fuck... my body is burning."

He starts moving his ass, pumping in pleasure through me. "Mine."

I gasp, letting the heat from his giant cock pulse through me. The bands on his cock rub against my walls, one after another, and my pussy takes him in more and more. I'm so stuffed and this is so amazing.

Maybe I should have let this happen long ago, maybe when he first pulled me onto his lap.

"You are such a meathead, big guy."

"Is that the way humans insult each other?" He takes a breath and picks up speed. "You are going to regret that."

"Oh! Fuck!" I scream as pleasure pumps into me. I clench onto his back, but he is so big that I can't hold him completely in my arms. He pounds in again and again until an orgasm explodes in me, sending my body tensing and shivering.

"You are so perfect for me. I told you to just like me already."

"Ha, do you really think that I'd fall in love with you like this? Geez, I have standards."

He groans. "You just love to be a tease."

"Show me what you got."

"Yes, sure. You get what you ask for."

I scream and moan in no time as his cock seems to grow even larger in me. Is that even possible?

Fuck!

He grabs my boobs and starts pinching my nipples. "Looks like these pink spots are the key, huh?"

My body is trembling from all the non-stop pleasure. I want to say something, but I can't make out a single word. All I can do is moan.

He fucks me so well. I've never felt something like this before.

He kisses me and his hot lips warm me. Maybe that's the only part of him that's soft. His tongue sneaks into me. The closeness between us should scare me, but I want this. I want him even though I should hate him.

But... Maybe he is trying to treat me well. I don't know about other times, but I know he fucks me well and I won't mind if he keeps doing it all the time.

His cock twitches in me and his strokes get longer and harder. With every long stroke, his cock gets larger and hotter. "Let me come inside you."

"Is that a question?"

He grunts and feels like he wants to chew me alive. "Yes. I hate you, but I'm going to ask."

"Asking nicely?"

"Yes..." He grinds his teeth with a low growl in his throat. His husky voice seems to make this even better. I think I like him, even though I don't understand him completely.

"Mmm! Yes! Fill me— Oh!" I shudder when he shoves his cock into the deepest of me. His cock twitches in me and pulses in his cum. I spread my legs even more, but as he fills me up, I can't stop shuddering. Maybe my body has been craving him.

His huge body presses against me as if he is trying to push me into the wall. He is so huge that... This is the first time I felt tiny, even tinier than I felt when there were a lot of uzains around me. We are naked and he has total control over me.

He grunts and his cock twitches even harder, giving me even more pleasure. "Serena... This is so good."

"Yes..." I hate to admit it, but who am I fooling?

"Good." He grins. I'm about to say something when he continues, "You have no idea. I'm so glad you're happy and satisfied."

Oh... He makes my heart swell. Maybe this is his way to please me and he is confident about his... ability to fuck me.

He taps my forehead with his horn. I reach up my tired and heavy hand to stroke his horn. He grins and seems to be happy about that. Maybe this is what he is trying, to show kindness. He's just not that much of a sweet talker.

He lets out another breath before he pulls out of me. My feet touch the floor and I almost fall. He grabs me again, holding me steadily and safely. "Did I fuck you so hard that you can't even stand?"

"Shut up..." I try, but my legs are weak. "That's only because you were holding my legs up and that hurts!"

He rubs my thighs. "Is this better?"

I take a breath. It would make me feel better if my legs were really numb, but they aren't. I'm tired from all the orgasms. Those were amazing, but they tired me out. I lick his chest when he is standing that close to me.

He groans. "What now? Do you think I'm your food?"

"Maybe." His skin is salty, probably from his sweat. "But you don't taste good."

He grunts. "Come on... I'm not for eating."

"Who knows?" I take a breath, trying to keep myself steady and stand on my own. "Are we going to shower or what?"

He eyes me up and down. "With how my cum is dripping out of you, maybe you really have to shower."

"Yes, you have to clean me now."

"No problem at all." He flexes his arm, showing off his muscles. I don't doubt he can clean me well with those strong arms.

And...

His cock dangles between his legs, still dripping my juice and his cum. He follows my gaze and his cock twitches. "Still want more?"

"Doesn't look like you can keep going."

He clicks his tongue. "Maybe I should be mad, but I can show you what else I can do if you are up for that."

Um... Maybe I won't want to know about that. If I let him keep going at me, I may regret it the next day. I shrug. "I'll spare you for now."

He laughs, so maybe suspects my real reason. My cheeks burn. "Shut up!"

"I said nothing." He spreads his hands to the side, pretending to be completely innocent even though I can see through his annoying ass.

I fold my arms when he winks and says, "Look, now you are shy and want to hide your boobs from me."

I hate him!

"Are we taking a shower or not? Maybe you should just get out of here so I can take a shower without your interruption."

"Fine, let's get showering." That's what he said, but...

Chapter 17

Vrek

My whole body burns, and even the shower water doesn't help it. The closer Serena is to me, the stronger the heat grows. The fire seems to be spreading along the markings on my body. I don't understand. The heat seems to be different.

My cock twitches as I put my hand that's soaked with body wash on her soft body. I take a breath, but it feels like my heart is about to jump out of my chest.

She lets out a soft moan as I rub the body wash on her. Maybe this isn't a good idea if we intend this to be a shower and for it to not morph into something else.

"Vrek... Do you clean yourself like that? Sloppily?"

I suck in a breath, but all I take in is her sweet scent. My cock twitches again, remembering how good her tight pussy felt. I want her and I want her now. I don't care that we just fucked, I want her again.

But I can feel that she is tired and I shouldn't keep doing it.

I roll my eyes at her. "Maybe you should stop making that cute voice and we can finish this the right way."

"Nothing has ever been right with you."

I suppose she isn't wrong. My hand moves to her pussy but she grabs my wrist. Her small hand can't even completely wrap around my wrist.

I ask, "What's about this?"

"Maybe we should clean ourselves instead." She looks serious with a light frown. Maybe she's thinking of something and... Is she thinking about how I kidnapped her again? I've already apologized!

But... Maybe it wasn't enough. Maybe I have to do something more before she will believe that I'm not trying to hurt her.

Okay... I can put in the effort if that's what I need to win her trust.

I nod. "Sure, if you prefer that, just so I'm not washing you *sloppily*."

She gives a weak smile and squirts some bodywash into her own hands.

I look away from her. Maybe I should control my erection, but when she's just a step away, it's tough.

I click the button for the water when we are ready. The warm water washes away the bodywash, but it doesn't wash away the remaining pleasure in me.

Should I ask? Will that be too much?

She seems oblivious to my thoughts and focuses on her body. It looks like she is done washing herself a lot sooner than me.

Now, she is the one watching me. "So, you're bigger than me and thus need more time?"

I roll my eyes. "It's because of you, always a distraction."

She chuckles and rubs my chest, which is still covered in a bit of bodywash. "Here you go, all cleaned up."

"That's what I call sloppy. Maybe you should clean my cock. Fuck..." I swear at once as she instantly starts stroking my cock. Like my wrist, she can't wrap her hand completely around my cock.

"Is this what you want?"

I let out a soft breath; my cock is getting hard again. "Unless you want to be fucked again, maybe you should stop."

She chuckles and finally lets go of me. "Fine, just be done washing yourself already."

She seems happy. I love her smile. Maybe threatening her really isn't the way. If I want to work with her and want her...

To be my mate?

My stomach squeezes at the thought. Is that what this is? Are we supposed to be together? Is that why I felt the heat spreading along my markings? There has to be something special.

She blinks as she looks at me. I hurry up to clean myself. Did she see something in my expression?

I stop the water and toss her a towel. I pick one up for myself, too. My eyes are locked on her. She isn't glancing at me though. Maybe she doesn't feel the heat like I do.

She has soft skin and no marking on her at all. I've met humans before, so none of that is very surprising, but it feels different when I meet Serena. I've never fucked a human before. But I doubt that has to do with her species. She has to be the reason.

"Vrek... Are you fine?"

"I'm perfectly fine."

"You look... Your mind seems to be elsewhere."

Everyone's been asking about that today... "Do you think so, too?"

"Looks to be. The intensity in your eyes is different."

I shrug and put on my trousers, picking up my belt. She also gets dressed, even though I prefer her naked.

When we get out to the cold and dark bedroom, I swear she lets out a soft breath. Is something wrong? Should I ask about that?

I'm used to doing whatever I want, but when it comes to her...

She climbs onto the bed, probably tired. Should I have carried her onto the bed? She isn't heavy for me to lift. Or should I just let it be?

Or maybe I should stop second-guessing myself.

Fuck... This is so hard.

I follow her onto the bed, getting comfortable on it. She stares at me. I roll around to her. The bed is a tiny bit too small since it was designed for a single uzain. At least she isn't that big.

My heart is hammering in my chest, but I make myself talk. "Looks like we have to make do with the room we get here."

"What do you mean?"

I wrap my hand around her and pull her to myself before I cover us with the blanket. Her body is so tempting.

She chuckles. "What is this about? You still haven't had enough?"

"You know I'll never have enough of you. But it looks like you should take a rest."

She huffs, still acting like a little brat.

"Here." I roll her over so I can pull her back to my chest. "Time to sleep."

"That's because you are too tired." That's what she said, but she soon yawns.

"I suppose you can imagine whatever you want."

I stroke her back. She will warm my bed, like I told her. Maybe she thinks that I'm the one warming her bed, but I don't care. She is mine and no one can change that.

Chapter 18

Vrek

When I open my eyes again, I almost jump.

I'm the only one in bed. Serena is gone!

I growl and get up. This isn't a good start to the day. Where is she?

"Serena?"

The silence in the room laughs at me.

I slam the button for the bathroom. But it opens to an empty room, not what I want to see.

I swear under my breath. Where the fuck is she?

I thought she already knew enough and wouldn't flee. Maybe I was wrong and she is going to prove to be more trouble than I expected.

My cock twitches. Now, I want to pin her down and fuck her so hard that she screams and begs for more.

I make sure I'm clothed before I dash out of the door. I have to find her.

I run down the corridor, running past a few uzains who are busy on their way to their shift. I don't even care to greet them.

"Vrek." One of them actually says something and I hate that.

I pause and get ready to shout at him when he says, "Are you in a hurry for the doughnuts? You're probably a bit too late."

What?

He chuckles. "If I were you, I'd run faster."

I huff and keep dashing down the corridor. Maybe he's just messing with me because I'm the one who brought Serena here.

Where can she be? The kitchen? But she hated having to make doughnuts for me.

Yet...

Before I turn the corner to the kitchen, I see uzains lining the corridor. What are they doing here? There shouldn't be anything to queue up for. More importantly, food is served in the food zone, which is even further away. Those beings serve food quickly, there's no reason...

Is that the secondary kitchen?

I arrive at the door of the kitchen and those who are lining up hiss at me. They are all flexed and ready to fight, probably thinking that I'm going to jump the queue and steal doughnuts.

The door is closed. I stop in front of it when one of the ones lining up grabs my shoulder. "Stop right there. You can't open the door like that."

"Why?" I growl at him.

"You are going to ruin everything! She said no peeking and no opening the door until the doughnuts are ready. Otherwise, it will ruin the magic."

So Serena tells everyone about the magic of creating doughnuts? I stare at the door. But... I thought she was making that stuff up to mess with me. Is that a real thing?

The one who growled at me continues, "Are you going to get in line now?"

I shake my head. "I'm not here for doughnuts. I'm just looking for Serena."

"Well, if you dare to steal a doughnut, I won't let you go just like that." He shows off his horns at me as if I'm going to ignore everyone who's waiting.

I hiss back at him and I show off my horns too. "Come on. I'm a male of my word." I take a step away from the door and stand to the side, away from these crazy guys. I'm just going to wait for the door to open. Serena should be fine, but I have to see her for myself

Behind me, there are angry gazes. Maybe they think that I'm trying to snag something.

I fold my arms and ignore that. No one can stop me from getting closer to Serena.

How could she do this to me? She didn't even tell me where she was heading.

It takes forever and a lot of foot-tapping before the door opens. I straighten up, but the ones in the line hiss at me and they pile into the kitchen.

But the first one halts and the rest run into each other, almost falling like bricks one after another. These stupid asses.

I don't usually hate my fellows, but these uzains annoy me.

It doesn't take long before they come out with doughnuts in their hands. They stare at the doughnuts as if they are precious coins or something. If they keep walking like that, they will run into a wall and I won't even feel sorry for them, they'd deserve it.

The line seems to be never-ending. I peek inside. I don't care whether anyone will shout at me, I'm going in.

There are growls behind me, but I ignore them.

Serena is inside and she is busy handing everyone doughnuts. The doughnuts smell amazing and they warm me before I have them.

She smiles at me as she hands another one to the next in line. "You're finally here."

What? I want to chat with her, but since there are others around, I don't want them to hear us.

The tray is soon empty, so Serena tells the rest of them to wait outside again.

There are groans from the disappointed uzains, which they deserve.

Serena frowns, probably feeling bad for them. "Well, come back later."

She picks up the pad of paper to the side, which she used to scribble the list of ingredients for me yesterday. "Can I have your names? You can come back later, and I'll have them ready for you. I didn't expect that everyone would be lining up for doughnuts."

The crazy ones are happy and they give their name, leaving Serena and I alone.

I fold my arms. "How could you leave me alone like that?"

"Hey, I told you I was heading here."

"No, you didn't. I woke up to the empty bed."

"Come on! You even told me you would be here soon. But your ass didn't show up until now."

I swear I don't remember that at all.

She snorts out a laugh. "Maybe you were too tired and fell asleep right after answering me."

I don't think she will lie to me about that. "Fine. Are you going to make more doughnuts?"

"I think so. It doesn't seem like I have anything else to do."

Is it too much to expect she has an extra for me?

She watches me for another moment before she turns to the oven. She opens the door and pulls out a tray. "Here."

She tosses me something and I hurry to catch it. It's a nice doughnut.

"So, you saved one for me."

"Yeah, I couldn't imagine how these guys are all so crazy for these, but I decided to keep one just in case. Consider yourself lucky I kind of like you."

I take a bite of the doughnut while it is still warm. I can let her tease me for a bit.

The doughnut almost melts in my mouth. This is the best thing I've ever eaten. I stare at it before taking another bite. "I think we need bigger doughnuts."

She chuckles. "Don't be greedy, okay?"

She moves to clean the utensils, seemingly already done with making doughnuts.

I ask, "Hey, I thought you said...?"

"I'll make more. Don't worry about that. Do you have a shift to go to?"

I scowl. The fact that I didn't even think about it sends my stomach sinking. "I... I will check, and maybe..."

"You better go. And finish your doughnut before leaving. I don't want the others to think I'm unfair."

I roll my eyes. "Come on. You are mine."

She chuckles.

I groan. "What? You know we are meant to be together."

She shrugs, and doesn't seem to care. "Maybe you should check your shift."

Fuck... If I'm supposed to be on shift and Captain catches me...

"Fine, I'll be back."

I leave the kitchen and rush my way over to the board with the schedule, which is closer than heading back to my room.

I halt right before I reach the board. Captain is standing right there, reading the board. Fuck...

He turns around at me and scowls. "Vrek, why are you here? Looking for me?"

I swallow. Does that mean I'm missing a shift and he is catching me wandering? What if he thought that I was distracted because of Serena? He would be mad and I wouldn't be able to keep her around. I shiver at the thought. I don't want to know what would happen to her if that happened. It wouldn't even be her fault.

His scowl grows and I better come up with something. My heart is racing and blood seems to freeze in me. "Captain... Well, yeah, I'm looking for you. Like, the human, she has started to make the doughnuts. That's the thing I want to tell you, so..."

He nods and the scowl is gone, so maybe he believes me. I didn't lie about most of that either, so... I hope it is fine.

He says, "Good, where is she?"

Fuck... Is he going to head there right now? When I left the kitchen, Serena was just done with making a batch and the next ones couldn't be ready this quickly. Would Captain be mad?

Before I look suspicious, I tell him she's in the kitchen.

Captain nods. "I'll check that out. Head back to the driving dashboard."

"Yes, Captain." Fuck... But maybe I dodged a bullet.

I turn around, planning to leave before he will give that more thought. I'm still not supposed to be here. Serena making doughnuts isn't an emergency and I could have waited for my shift to end to tell him.

"Vrek."

Fuck...

"Yes, Captain."

He lifts his brows at me. "Is the woman staying in your room?"

I swallow with a fire exploding in me. Does he mean to take her away from me? I know he is the captain and he sets the rules, but at the same time, I don't want to and I won't let anyone take Serena away from me.

The heat spreads from my stomach to the rest of my body, following the markings on me. It burns so hot that it hurts. I should slow myself, but it is hard.

Do I need to fight for her?

I nod. "Yes."

Captain narrows his eyes. "You know that we aren't supposed to have a female here."

"I thought we discussed this before I brought her to the ship."

"Yes, we did. We didn't discuss where she would stay though."

I resist the urge to show off my horns. Captain is a very experienced warrior. It will be a tough battle to win. "I suppose... She likes to stay with me though."

"Really? Why's that? What did you do to her?"

Fuck... Since there hasn't been any female on the spaceship, there isn't a rule about no fucking on the ship. Technically, I can fuck Serena however I want as long as she wants that too. But practically, I know I probably shouldn't. Yet, Serena... She sends warmth through my body like no one else.

I shake my head. "Nothing. We just share things about our very different lives." Does this sound like a decent enough excuse?

He watches me up and down. "I'll talk to her."

Except I want to punch him and tell him to get out of the way. Maybe I shouldn't tell him that. But then I would have it bad.

Dammit...

He walks off. I want to kick him. But I probably shouldn't do that. I hate this. If I were the captain, it would be a lot easier.

This male in front of me barely has more experience and years working on a spaceship than I do. I have strong horns and muscles too. And I can fight amazingly well. It isn't like he's that much better than me.

I silently sigh and turn to the driving dashboard, that is probably better, at least for now.

Serena...

My marking burns even harder now. Maybe that means that I have to fight for her, to keep her with me.

Mine.

Chapter 19

Serena

I check the oven, making sure the timer is set. I don't mind making doughnuts for these guys. Probably. Maybe they aren't that bad.

How Vrek pinned me to the wall and fucked so well that...

Fuck... I shouldn't think about that.

My cheeks are burning and they're probably so red that it's embarrassing.

There is a low hiss of the door. I've already told everyone that I need solitude for the doughnuts to work and they have been believing that. So...

"Vrek?"

"No."

I spin around at the deeper and more powerful voice. It is the captain, so no wonder he came in regardless. Maybe those waiting outside told him, and maybe he saw the note I stuck on the door, but he ignored those. I doubt any of the uzains would dare to stop the captain.

What should I say?

He looks around and stares at the oven. "When will they be ready?"

"Soon?"

He snarls.

I check the timer on the oven. "Another ten minutes before I can fry them."

"Good." He comes over, getting closer and closer. I fight the urge to take a step back. He is a huge guy and I'm not sure what he wants.

He lifts his brows. "Where are you going?"

"Um... Nowhere? Do you know that..."

"The doughnuts need solitude?" He snorts what sounds like a laugh, but his face is so serious that I don't even dare to joke. "I don't deal with stupidity. There's no such thing."

Did he see through it? All the others believed it though.

He grabs my collar and yanks me off the floor. He hisses. "Maybe you should realize everything on this spaceship is mine and that includes you."

I flinch. Vrek yanked me off the floor before, but he hadn't been this scary. It feels like this captain wouldn't hesitate killing me if he has to, or even... if he wants to. Maybe this is what the captain of the dangerous bandit gang is capable of. And maybe this is his way to manage and control all these huge uzains.

He leans even closer. "You seem scared."

My lips are trembling even though I wish to keep that at bay.

He leans even closer, so close that his hot breath lands on me as if he is sniffing me, getting ready to put me on the table for dinner. "Have you been lying to me?"

"I..."

"Human, if I were you, I'd be very careful. Vrek seems to like you."

Fuck... Is he here because of that? Because he thinks that he is the captain and he isn't happy with how I'm staying in Vrek's room? Vrek mentioned that no females are allowed, so...

He hisses at my face.

If...

I roll my eyes. "No way. You kidnapped me and forced me out of my life. Even if he likes me, I hate him."

The world in front of me spins and a shadow approaches. I gasp and close my eyes. Waiting for him to smack my head into the wall.

I shudder, anticipating my crushed skull and blood. It takes seconds before my head taps the wall.

But it doesn't hurt.

I open my eyes to find my head against the wall. The captain is still watching me.

He says, "I'm telling you: you are disposable here. If you interrupt this spaceship and my rules, I'll kill you."

I gasp at that. Maybe he means to scare me, but for now...

"I won't ever try that. I don't care about your..."

He growls at me. "What did you say?"

"Wait! I mean, I won't interrupt anything. I'll just stay here and make doughnuts."

There is a ding from the oven. Captain looks over there. "So, the doughnuts are ready."

"But you have to be outside first."

"Why?" He glances at the oven. "There's no magic in food preparation."

"Are you sure about that?"

He glares at me, interrogating me with his gaze. His hand moves slowly, tapping my head on the wall.

It's probably too late to admit that I lied. I can't go back, but if I'm not careful enough... "Are you sure you know about all the food? From all cultures? All species?"

He still doesn't seem convinced at all. His grip on me is tight with no hint of easing.

I continue, "Maybe you should put me down. If we miss the timing for the doughnuts, they won't be as good as they can be."

He sneers at me. I wince, waiting for him to smash me into the wall.

But moments later, he puts me down. He hisses, "If I find out you lied, you'll regret it. Get those ready and give me some before I'm done waiting."

Okay... So, he believes me?

"I'll try to be quick, but good things take time."

He lifts his brows, silently hushing me and demanding I be honest. I shiver at that. It's hard not to get worried when I can die at any time. Maybe making doughnuts for them for a while isn't that bad.

He finally heads to the door.

I add, "You also can't peek."

"If the magic that that good, it should figure out how to work regardless."

"Magic is magic."

He says nothing but keeps heading to the door. When he finally leaves, I almost slump onto the floor. I clench onto the kitchen island with my heart hammering even harder in my chest. My throat is tight and it feels like I'm choking to death, even though Captain is already gone.

I close my eyes, chanting to myself that it is going to be fine. I have no idea whether it is really going to be fine, but at least I'm not dead.

I open the door of the oven, pulling out the tray with the baking gloves on. The doughnuts are fine. The oven turns off on its own anyway. All I have to do is to dip them into the icing, which is part of the magic.

Where is Vrek? Is he on duty now?

He probably is, otherwise, he would be back. But I told him about the magic too, so maybe he's waiting outside.

I glance at the door. From the window on it, it seems like Captain isn't peeking. He probably figured that he didn't have to. It isn't like I can escape the ship just like that.

The doughnuts are all on the tray, looking pretty and smelling great. I smile, despite the tension still strong in me. I believe in bakery magic too. Happy beings bake better than upset and angry ones. I don't have a reason or theory behind that, but I know it's the case.

Whether these uzains believe in that or not, I'm going to insist on that. It's just not the kind of magic that... will require Vrek to stand on one foot while mixing the ingredients.

I toss every pan and mixing bowl into the sink. Do I take more time here and pretend I'm doing the magic for a longer while? Or do I do this quickly like the Captain demands?

Is Vrek here? At least he knows a bit more about Captain than I do. That uzain is scary.

I take a deep breath, but it isn't helping. My heart is still racing and my hands are shaking. I close my eyes, but that does nothing.

The kitchen feels tiny and it feels like the walls are coming together and they will squeeze me flat and crush me. No matter how impossible that is, it still grows the load in my stomach.

It's going to be fine. Unless Captain finds something solid, he is probably not going to kill me. Hopefully...

I swallow, fighting the urge to barge out of the door and hide somewhere. Even if I want to flee, Captain is right at the door. There's no way to flee. I open the door before I stop myself. May as well...

As soon as the door opens, a shadow hovers over. It is Captain towering over with his menacing glare. "So, you are done with the doughnuts."

I nod. "Yeah, it's a bit tough to pull off the magic when my hands keep shaking, but—"

He grabs me and I'm not the only one gasping. A few uzains nearby, who are waiting for doughnuts, are probably also gasping. I bet they won't want me dead, but if Captain wants to kill me, none of them will do a thing to help me.

He leans closer. "Are you blaming me for that?"

I shake my head as quickly as I can without straining my neck. "Not at all. Maybe my hands are just tired from making all the doughnuts."

"You better get over it, otherwise, I'll have no use for you." He looks into the kitchen. None of the uzains dare to step past him into the kitchen.

Captain shoves me to the side. I stumble to not fall to the floor when he heads into the kitchen. He doesn't even care what happens to me.

The other uzains watch, but none come up to help. They are frowning deeply and seem to want to help, but maybe none of them dare when it is Captain who pushed me to the side.

I don't blame them... He's scary.

I hold onto the wall to keep standing. Captain is inside and is munching down on the doughnuts. I suppose he likes those.

There are a dozen doughnuts, but... soon, there are only two left on the tray while Captain has two in his hand. He glances at the ones lined up and waiting, then at the two doughnuts in his hands. He puts one back on the tray and leaves with one.

He walks past me and whispers, "It looks like you have things to say."

"You are a mean and bad..." I bite my tongue before I end up saying even more. I shouldn't even start, but when it comes to it... I just can't stop myself.

"A bad what?"

I look away from him, but he hisses, making me continue my sentence. "A bad... captain."

I wince at that, waiting for him to kill me or hurt me. There is no way he will let me slide with that. He just warned me about his rules and how I should never overstep.

The rest of the uzains are in the kitchen, hopefully dividing the doughnuts peacefully instead of fighting over them. No one is going to care about what is going to happen to me. They may miss the doughnuts, but that won't hurt them enough for them to want to save me.

But Captain laughs. "You are funny." He snorts out another laugh. "Look, I can let that slide this time, but you'll be spending the night with me."

What?

His eyes are dark and he doesn't seem to be joking. He strokes my cheek, but someone dashes in between Captain and me.

"What is going on here!" It is Vrek and he growls at Captain, shoving him to the side.

"Fuck!" He hisses when Captain punches him in the stomach.

"No!" I yell and try to get between them, but Vrek pushes me to the side and swings his fist at Captain.

Captain snorts and dodges, but Vrek slams into him with his horns. Captain grabs his horn, but Vrek kicks him so hard that Captain stumbles a few steps away.

Before they crash into each other again, I stand between them. "Stop it!"

Both of them are sneering at each other, and it is so dumb to be standing here.

Captain grunts. "What's your issue?"

Is that a question for me? Or is that for Vrek?

Vrek says, "What are you doing to her?"

Captain rolls his eyes. "I do what I want. Since she wronged me, she has to make it up to me and she will be spending the night with me."

Vrek growls and moves. I spread my arms, wrapping them around him and stopping him. He is squealing and growling, grabbing my waist as if he wants to shove me to the side but he doesn't want to hurt me. "No, she's not spending the night with you, never!"

Captain folds his arms with a razor-sharp glare that can kill. "Brave for you to try and fight me."

"I'm going to do that until you stop bothering her!"

"Everything on this spaceship is mine."

Vrek growls and doesn't seem to care. "Shut the fuck up! I don't care what you said. Serena isn't yours."

Captain comes over and grabs my arm. "You can think whatever you want."

Fuck... The captain yanks on my shoulder, pulling me from Vrek while Vrek wraps his arm around my waist and snatches Captain's hand.

"Don't touch her!"

I have to get out of here before they fight again and catch me in the crossfire. Captain throws a fist at Vrek's face, but he just stands right there and takes the hit. He screeches, but... he took it for me. If he had dodged...

"Vrek!"

"No!"

A few other uzains come over and they grab Vrek's arms, yanking them off me. Captain pulls me to him and snorts a laugh at Vrek. "Time for you to learn your place. Lock him out of here, I don't want to see his face."

Fuck! I don't want this!

I'm not anyone's!

I pull my arm away and halt. "No, I'm not going with you."

Captain turns around, grabs my throat, and shoves me up against the wall, all in one swift motion.

I groan when pain spreads through me. It hurts, but I can still open my eyes.

He says, "If I were you, I would learn to be a bit smarter."

I grab onto his hand at my throat. His big hand might squeeze me to death, but... I gasp and it feels like his grip gets stronger. "No... I'm not spending the night with you."

"Except you're not the one picking and choosing. Come over before I'll make you."

There are screams and shouts behind me. These uzains are dragging Vrek to the side, and they are going down the corridor to the other side, soon moving out of my vision. There is fear in Vrek's eyes and that hurts.

An arm wraps around my waist. I spin around only to have the Captain's hand on my throat again.

He hisses. "What are you looking at? Drop that one. Vrek is just one of the many uzains, not worth your time."

I... I don't know what to think. I should hate Vrek when he kidnapped me. But Captain was the one approving that. Every one of these uzains is here to get things out of me and they are going to do whatever it takes. And now... are they fighting over me?

He strokes my throat with a finger. "Come with me."

But I don't want to...

I already agreed to make doughnuts for them, but guess that's not going to be enough for them. "No."

"What?"

"What are you going to do to Vrek?"

"I haven't decided about that. Looks like you care about him. "

"He kidnapped me."

"Well, if you hate him that much, we can kill him. You can keep the horns if you want."

What the actual fuck? Is he...

What is happening here? This place is crazy!

I shake my head. "No. Are you really going to kill him just like that?"

"He defied me and tried to fight me. Maybe it will be helpful for you to learn what will happen if you go against me. I can kill you off the same way."

"You are such a monster."

"There is a lot more I can do to you, to prove how much a monster I am."

I shake my head. "I don't care about that. I don't want to have anything to do with any of you."

"I don't care." He growls and my knees go weak.

He comes over to me. I stumble back, but my legs refuse to move. He grabs me and pulls me down the corridor even though I fight to resist him. I trip and fall, but he doesn't care and he drags me on the floor.

He hisses as he keeps walking with wide strides. "You can scream and shout, but no one will help you."

Fuck!

Chapter 20

Vrek

"Let go of me!" I kick and yank my arms out of the two who are grabbing me, but they grab me again soon enough. There are too many of them for me to win against.

"Vrek, come on... What are you even doing? Do you think that it is a good idea to fight against Captain like that?"

"He fucking took Serena from me!"

They look at each other, and don't even seem to care. They pull me all the way down the corridor despite the shouts I hear echoing. Maybe Serena is arguing with Captain, but... I'm not sure how she will make it out. I only hope she won't be hurt.

We arrive at the chamber to lock up invaders or whoever the Captain decides. Now, the four of them shove me into the room and the door closes behind me.

It's dark here, and cold. I know there is nothing here. No bed, no chair, nothing. I take a few steps inside, sitting against the wall. Who knows what will happen to me?

Before I ran to fight Captain, all I saw was him grabbing Serena as if he wanted to kill her off. Maybe he didn't like the doughnuts or maybe Serena did something that pissed him off. Serena can be a brat at times, which... I already warned her about that and how if she kept acting like that, it wouldn't be good for her, yet...

Wait... Maybe instead of her, I should worry for myself.

I rub my temple and sigh. I hate how useless I am. I didn't manage to save Serena, and I'm not doing anything that will make things easier for myself either. I'm such a useless uzain.

Maybe Serena will like the captain more. But...

My stomach churns and I want to puke. It hurts to keep thinking about her. I just want her to be fine. The heat in me might explode at any second. I want her. Serena and I are meant to be together. I feel it in me growing stronger since I met her and I pinned her against the wall in the bathroom. She wanted me, too.

I grit my teeth and run my hand along my horn. I have to do something, but there's no way to open the door from the inside.

Serena... Fuck... I hate myself so much...

Chapter 21

Serena

I arrive at a room that's larger than Vrek's. It's a tidy room, but at the same time, it's...

Captain watches me with a proud grin on his face. "My room is a lot better. And I'm the Captain."

I go up to him. He doesn't seem to care. Maybe one day I will stop putting myself in danger, but at the same time...

Maybe like Vrek said, I'm a brat.

"Fuck!" he growls as I kick him squarely in the crotch. Before he straightens, I yank his laser gun off his belt and point it at him.

He hunches over with an ugly scowl. "What the fuck!"

"I've told you. I don't want to be here." My hands shake, but not enough for me to drop the gun.

I would have done the same with Vrek, but he was never geared, so there was no gun for me to grab.

He straightens and huffs. "Brave, huh?"

"I'm just making myself clear. I'm not going to stay here and I'm not spending the night with you."

He rolls his eyes. "That's not the point. Give the gun back."

"Do I look that stupid?"

"No, you don't. But I'm not going to do what you have in mind either."

"I don't trust you."

"Same. I don't trust you either."

I'm confused. But him being the captain means that I have to be even more careful. "I deserve to have something to defend myself with."

He watches me for another second before he shrugs. "You don't deserve anything just for existing, but fine, you can keep that. For now."

Huh? Maybe that means he has another gun or two, which I don't doubt.

He folds his arms. "I'm not going to let Vrek insult me in front of everyone."

"You said you wanted me to spend a night with you before Vrek even showed up."

"Don't care. Whoever dares to test the line will be punished. No one shall even think about attempting that."

"What do you want? Just be clear. I don't want to play games with you. I have no interest in your politics."

He snorts out a laugh without even smirking. "It doesn't matter what you said. Your existence is causing me trouble."

I frown at that. It's just dumb. "Tell me what I've done."

"Exist. Those uzains like you a bit too much."

So... He is worried that I'm affecting his position on the spaceship?

I shrug. "No, they don't. What they care about is the doughnuts. If they cared, they'd have helped me when you cornered me."

"They haven't yet. But if I allow you to continue to exist here, they will."

I roll my eyes. "I don't even care about that. Do you really think I'm going to organize them to overthrow you or something? Geez, that's so dumb."

He doesn't seem to care. "More importantly, Vrek seems to think that you're his."

"No way! I'm not anyone's."

"Good." He lifts his brows for the first time. Maybe this is what he wants? And... Maybe he isn't looking to make me his? Like, whatever the fuck that's supposed to mean.

He comes closer, even though I lift the gun at him. He snickers. "Shoot me, otherwise, you may as well give me the gun."

I swallow and point the gun at myself instead. "Maybe this will go better for me." Will he make me do it? I want nothing to do with him. A jealous and possessive monster...

He tilts his head to the side. "Interesting. That only makes you even more dangerous. Give me the gun. I won't hurt you as long as you listen to me."

"Your rules change all the time and I'm not going to trust you."

"They like the doughnuts too much and soon, they will like you for that."

"I can't control that. You're the one who wanted me to make the doughnuts, but when I did exactly that, you weren't happy."

"There is only one solution for that."

Fuck...

He continues, "You'll be mine, then none of them will think of something else."

"No!" I scream back at him. Maybe I should pull the trigger, except... I've done so much to stay alive in front of these monsters. "You just said you won't do that."

"Give me the gun and we'll talk."

I remain glaring at him and clenching tightly on the gun. I'm not going to trust him that easily.

He says, "Look, I won't hurt Vrek if that's what you're worried about."

"Except if I do as you say, you're going to think that I care about Vrek. Then you'll be mad about it. You hate it when he has what you don't."

"Does he? Does he have you? Are you his? Did you lie to me?"

I shake my head. "No, I'm not anyone's. I don't like Vrek. I don't like any of you here. All I want is to be safe."

"Give me the gun."

"No."

He takes back his hand. "If you love my gun, you can keep it. And..." He eyes me up and down, but he shrugs. "I'm not someone like that. I don't take a female just because I can. You'll get your room for the night and you shall stay there instead of Vrek's room."

So... All he wants is...

He says, "I told you. I won't let anyone insult me without punishment. I don't care about you. You will be hurting Vrek if... if he thinks you're his, which... unless you're lying to me..."

I let out a breath. "I can only hope you aren't lying to me."

"It is okay. You can take your time. You have to be smart to operate a cafe before you are here. Use your brain and act smartly. This is your warning. If anything is off, I won't let you go just like this."

I scowl at him. "What will you do to Vrek?"

He muses. "I haven't decided on that. I didn't expect him to show up when I talked to you. And he was supposed to be on shift, so..."

"Don't hurt him because of me."

"Why do you care about him? He had you for a night and..."

"I don't think it is fair to him. All I did was kick his ass and his balls."

"Just like you did to me?"

"Seeing as you're the captain, I kicked even harder."

He snorts a laugh. "Interesting. For that..."

Before I can blink, he snatches my throat, squeezing so hard that I can't hold onto the gun. It drops on the floor. I kick him, but when I can't even breathe, I can't hurt him.

After a second, he drops me to the floor. "This is your punishment for what you did. Come with me."

I gasp. The world is still spinning and my head is still blank. My legs are weak and I can't seem to stand.

He stops at the door, watching me with a light frown. "Humans are that fragile, huh?"

I look away from him. I hate this place.

He comes over and I close my eyes. He nudges me with his fucking feet. "Can you walk?"

"I can't breathe."

"Well..."

He looks around and shrugs. "Whatever. If you can't walk, you'll stay here for the night. I don't mind."

No! I don't want to—

Before I scream at him, he heads to the door and leaves.

What does that even mean?

Maybe he is out there looking for a few other uzains to carry out his plan, whatever that is. He said I should go to another room, so maybe he is looking for another uzain to make me go.

I lean on the wall behind me. I hate this place. This is so stupid.

These uzains have never cared to explain themselves. I don't even care about what they think. I just want to be with Vrek and make sure he is fine.

Wait...

I shake my head, trying to clear my mind. I'm waiting for a chance to get the hell out of here and maybe try to go back to my old life. I'm not here to stay with Vrek or making them doughnuts.

I just sit there, too tired to stand. What will Captain do when he gets back?

But he isn't back.

My heart skips a beat. What if he is heading to Vrek... to deliver his punishment?

Fuck...

I never meant to cause anyone any trouble. Even if I don't like Vrek, I still don't want him to be in trouble.

I suppose I don't have to care. But Vrek only got into trouble because he was worried about me and wanted to protect me. I close my eyes, and how he annoyed me flashes in my mind. And at the same time, when I let him pin me to the wall, and let him have his way to me, it wasn't that bad.

A stream of heat reaches my cheek. Maybe I shouldn't like that this much, but who am I fooling?

I rub my temple. Captain isn't back. I can only hope he isn't torturing Vrek. I clench my fist, fighting to stop myself from shaking.

I push against the floor to stand. Whatever Captain thinks, I'm going to do what I want to do. If he told me to stay here, I'd be right on his bed.

Maybe this is his plan and he will be back and do stupid things to me, but...

Hm... The gun I held is still on the floor. Did he leave that there? For me? Or did he forget about it?

I pick it up regardless. If he dares to make me do things or does things to me, I'm going to fire at him. Even if he is going to hurt me, I won't make it easy for him.

This is the first time I've had the whole bed for myself. I spread my arms and legs, taking up space. If Captain thinks he is the boss here, I'm going to mess with him.

Chapter 22

Serena

When I open my eyes, I'm on a bed, alone. I sit up to find... I'm still alone. The gun I put next to the pillow is still there.

What does this mean?

The room seems to be the same way as when the captain left. Did he come back? Or... Did he go to the other room instead, leaving me here for the night?

I head to the door. He told me to stay in the room for the whole night, but the night is over now, so I shouldn't have to...

The door opens before I press the button. I take a step back before I can run into...

"Captain."

"Yes, it looks like you're done listening to me. Feeling confident now?" He still looks the same. His menacing glare is on point, threatening to tear me into pieces. I hate that, but at the same time, maybe I should shut up for another moment.

He gestures for me to give way and for him to go inside. I refuse and remain standing there. He turns his head to the side, showing off his horns. "What's in your head, human?"

"I have a name."

"Are you going to answer my question?"

"I want to get out of here and I want to make sure Vrek is doing well. While I don't really care for someone who kidnapped me, at least he tried to protect me from an angry monster."

He lifts his eyebrows at me. "Are you calling me a monster?"

"Yes, and I'm being nice."

He watches me for another moment. Do I look away or something? But I do hate what he did.

I swallow. Maybe I should stay quiet, but... "How's Vrek doing? Where were you?"

"Did you wish I was there with you for the night instead?"

I clench a fist. He glances at my hand almost at once. He says, "If that's a threat, I'm not scared. You can't pull the same trick on me twice."

"I thought you agreed to leave me alone if I made the doughnuts."

"I can't have Vrek thinking he is better than me when he can have something I don't have."

"Such a big ego. He has never thought about that. All he cares about is doughnuts."

"Maybe." He shrugs, and I doubt he even heard what I said. All he cares about is what he dreams up in his mind. "Are you going to stay in the room I assign you?"

"So, you are here to bring me there."

"Yes. Or would you rather...?"

Maybe that room won't be that bad. "This is your plan for Vrek to stop thinking I'm his."

"Yes. I hope you will understand."

I guess I can't disagree with him. Maybe I also shouldn't argue, and it's going to be better for me. It isn't like I'm dead set on staying in Vrek's room either. Why would I be?

"Okay, I'll stay there if that eases your huge ego."

"You really should learn how to talk with more respect."

I lift my brows at him. Except I don't think I'm going to learn that anytime soon. "You have never considered me one of your fleet. You love to think that I'm a slave here."

"So, you want to be considered one of us."

"I want to be treated with respect."

"I can give you some if you know what to do."

"I'm not going to suck your cock for that."

He laughs. This is probably the first time I saw him laugh. Even if he is laughing at me and probably thinking I'm an idiot, maybe this is better than his glare.

It isn't like I'm here to make him like me anyway.

I hate every one of these uzains.

After he is done laughing, he clears his throat. "Let's get going."

I follow him. He is a huge male who is even more capable than Vrek to kill me. More importantly, Vrek cares about me. At least he seems to. When he held me close to him as we slept together on his bed, he was gentle, and... it felt like he treasured me and wanted to keep me with him.

We arrive at a room. He points at the number card above the button for the door. "This is your room. Other than the kitchen and the other public areas, I expect you to be here."

I shrug. "Sure, it isn't like I want to be somewhere else anyway."

"Good."

He turns around, already leaving. I take a step and insert myself between him and the door. "Where is Vrek?"

"Why are you asking about him?"

"I know you don't want me to care about him, but he got into trouble because of me."

"He is fine. Punished, but not dead."

Can I trust him?

He seems to see my thoughts and he clears his throat. "I'm the captain. You have my word. I'm not looking forward to losing warriors left and right either."

I suppose... That's the same reason these won't hurt me: they want doughnuts.

He lifts his eyebrows at me. "So, are you going to get out of my way?"

I take a step to the side. I suppose it will make things easier for the future if I don't keep fighting him over this. He has to want the doughnuts too, and that may be one of my very limited bargaining chips.

He leaves without saying another word. I need the time to regroup and organize my thoughts. Maybe this is even harder than running a cafe and making sure it stays profitable.

I hope Vrek is fine.

Chapter 23

Vrek

It's cold. I can almost smell my death. The low humming noise of the engine is still here. The floor seems to hum along to it, vibrating slightly.

Does that mean I'm still alive?

My horns hurt.

My whole body hurts.

I'm on the floor and I'm too tired to move a single inch. I gasp, taking in the scent of my own blood.

Fuck...

I take another breath, but choke on my own blood.

It is fine. I'm not dead.

How is Serena?

Is she fine?

Captain grabbed her, and who knows what he did to her?

He wasn't gone for long. Or maybe time felt weird since I'm locked into this room. There is nothing that marks the passage of time. All I knew is I remained sitting against the wall for longer than I wanted. Before that, I remained on the floor for longer than I remembered.

Captain was back and he whipped me. I supposed that was appropriate for what I did earlier in the day. I wasn't expected to fight him. But I couldn't stop myself. What if he hurt Serena?

Fuck... I hate how useless I am. I'm still alive, but what about her?

The captain would hate for me to feel something for her. I know that and I told Serena about that too. But maybe just because she stayed in my room for the night, Captain thought I felt something for her and she would affect the dynamics on the ship.

That is so dumb. All of us know that he is the captain and I don't think anyone is going to think any differently even if Serena stays here with us.

I miss her.

If only...

I guess the only way for this to be fine is for me to be the captain, which I'm not and I won't be for a long time. I just want to know that she is fine. I've never felt so strongly for someone before. It feels like she and I are meant for each other. I want her to be happy here and I want to be happy with her. I know I'm probably not the strongest male on the spaceship, but maybe...

Serena is a human, so maybe she doesn't care about being mated to the strongest male in the territory. I wish I was that one, but I wasn't. There are rules I have to follow. But...

This isn't even fair.

Captain doesn't care about her either. All he cares about is his status, which I don't care for.

Would he want to take her as his mate? Just because he is the captain? Or maybe not as his mate, but just a toy?

I shiver at the thought. The pain in my body and the faint taste of blood in my mouth don't seem that bad. It hurt a ton more when I couldn't do anything to protect her.

There is a low hiss of the door opening. Maybe Captain is back again and I'm going to be punished again.

I close my eyes, waiting for him to growl at me.

But seconds passed with nothing happening. I turn around, as much as I can before it hurts.

Someone is running to me. The room is too dark for me to see who that is. Before I can grunt, someone holds me in their arms.

It... It is Serena. I will always remember her scent. More importantly... "Serena!"

"Vrek! How are you?"

"What are you even doing here?"

She can't be here. Maybe I'm dreaming.

She strokes my back. "Hey, what happened to you?"

I grunt and while I want to look strong in front of her, I can't. I want her to hold me and I want to taste her lips.

"Hey, be quick." It is Zil's voice. Maybe he is here to help so Serena can get out of here in time. Otherwise, she would be locked up here with me and Captain isn't blind.

She sighs. "Okay, at least you aren't dead. I was so worried." She... She kisses me. But before I can kiss her back, she moves away. I know she is in a hurry and for it to be safe for both of us and also Zil, she has to cut it short. But I... I miss her and I want to be alone with her.

Something touches my lips, but it isn't her lips. It's warm and soft, though.

She rubs my horn and lets go of me. "Eat something, okay?"

Before I can talk, the light from the opened door is gone. She left...

I sniff as a tear runs down my cheek. I reach for what's in my mouth. Hm... Warm and... there is dust on it.

Wait!

I take a bite at the thing. It is dark enough that I can't see what that is, but now that my heartbeat has slowed down, I can smell things again. It's a soft and perfect doughnut. And that's not dust, it's powdered sugar.

I munch down and it disappears quicker than I want. It is sweet and warms me from the inside, so much more than other food can do. It's even better than when my fleet won fights and we got to share the loot.

The doughnut does a lot more than everything else. I want her. Just the two of us.

I stare at the darkness in front of me again.

Fuck... While Serena looks and sounds fine, I know something happened... She... Captain's scent is on her. He must have put her on his bed, and who knows what else?

I grit my teeth. It feels like my horns are aching. If I made it clearer that I want Serena as my mate, would anything have changed for the better?

Maybe not...

Maybe all that would do is make Captain even angrier at us.

What should I do?

I want to get out of here, but I can't even do that. Maybe I'm the most useless uzain who ever existed, and not worthy of Serena...

Chapter 24

Serena

I suck in a deep breath as I watch Captain shove another few doughnuts into that annoying big mouth that is still moving. His breathing noise annoys me beyond imagination. I hate him and I think he knows that.

It's been another day. I didn't dare to go to Vrek again. I already bothered Zil, and that may make him the next one on the receiving end of Captain's rage.

I've been in the cafeteria all the time I'm not in the kitchen. I've not seen Vrek at all. The other uzains are still nice to me, but it feels like everyone has been dodging me and worrying that if they even talk to me a bit too long, they'll be punished.

I hate this. What's with this place? School and college with stupid drama and popularity contests all the time? This is some stupid hierarchy play which I don't want to be involved in. These uzains are all immature—

I blink and fight to yank my mind elsewhere. Captain may as well be reading me. I may not be as good at controlling my face as I hope and I don't need the risk.

He says, "These feel different."

"What do you mean?"

He stares at the half in his hand. "I don't know. You're supposed to be making the good doughnuts."

Compared to their stupid bread, this is great. I take one and tear a bite to try it out. It smells and tastes the same, even the texture feels the same. This is the type of doughnut that is one of the bestsellers. After making these for years, I don't make mistakes anymore, if at all. When I started, there were times when some batches weren't good enough, but not now, and not this lot.

I shrug. "I don't understand what you mean. This is as good as the ones I made before."

He glares at me, seemingly dead set on the doughnuts being different. "Did anyone mess around when you were doing the magic for these?"

Oh... So he also believes me on that, huh? Good for me.

I shrug. "I'm not sure. The doughnuts can be sensitive."

"Aren't you supposed to know when you are the one doing the magic?"

Fuck... Is he testing me? "Yes and no. If something is majorly wrong, I will know. But it is magic, so it isn't like any being has ever completely understood that, got it?"

He muses and takes another bite of the doughnut. "Interesting."

"Did you peek when I was preparing the doughnuts?"

He rolls his eyes. "No. I'm just wondering what messed these up."

Maybe uzains are a lot more sensitive to taste. "Who knows?"

He watches me and eyes me up and down. "I suppose the only thing that's different between the two lots of doughnuts is..."

Vrek was locked up and probably tortured some more.

Nausea surges in me and it feels like I may die from the pain in my stomach. I don't want Vrek to be hurt because of me, whether I like him or not. But... I know some say that mood affects the food I make. I've never given that serious attention. Good days or bad, I work in the cafe and I bake everything, and customers are always happy.

Maybe Captain is assuming something and he feels what he imagined in his ego-driven big head with no brain.

But... I can only hope his thoughts won't lead to more suffering for Vrek.

He comes closer after he finishes the bite in his hand. "Look, it seems like you are worried about him."

"He tried to help me. It's hard not to worry about him."

"Hmm... So, you want me to free him."

"I think you've punished him already."

He lifts my chin and makes me look him in the eyes. "Do you love him?"

"Hell no!" Why would I like someone like Vrek? Let alone love him? All he did was kidnap me, make me make doughnuts, add trouble to my plate, annoy me, and... fuck me...

Captain tilts his head to the side. "If you'll behave, I'll free him."

I spread my hands to the side. "I'm behaving. I have been doing all the things you told me. You are the one who isn't satisfied with the doughnuts. I told you I'd done my best and all I could. The magic has its own moving parts which no one can completely control."

He huffs and heads to the door. "Make me more."

"And what will I get for that?"

He glances at me. "Looks like you enjoy testing me. I shouldn't let you succeed."

I fold my arms. "You are the one who loves to test me. It doesn't have to be like this."

"You should be listening to me and stop acting like a brat. That's how things work on this spaceship."

"So, you're the dictator here, huh? Get to do whatever you want no matter how dumb it is?"

"Well, I'm reasonable."

"No, you aren't. Vrek thought you wanted to kill me, and that was why he ran in and stood between us."

"I know. But he still doesn't get to fight me."

"What else was he supposed to do? Stand to the side like the others?"

He watches me with his cold eyes. "Yes. The others know not to defy me."

"I think Vrek is better. He knew I needed help. I also know you hate that."

"You have to understand how hard it is to make sure everyone is doing what they are supposed to."

"All they do is to let you act as if you are better than everyone. And maybe threaten to hurt me."

"You better learn to control your mouth."

"I'm bad at saying nothing when I need to say something."

He says nothing and leaves. I hope that's because he is getting tired of me.

The empty tray stares back at me. He hoards every-thing for himself. He says it is to make sure the dough-nuts are safe for consumption, but both of us know that's just an excuse. All of the doughnuts are safe and some uzains already enjoyed them before Captain's ass barged in and interrupted everything.

Someone just has to act as if he is important.

I gather the ingredients again. Maybe he likes the doughnuts, but it's impossible for him to consume an-other entire dozen. I don't mind making some for every-one if it means I will get a better chance to get out of here when it comes down to it.

Vrek was nice to me, and Zil risked a lot to help me, but I can't stay here if it might get worse for them. And I can't stand that ego-head bastard.

I'll make more doughnuts, at least for now.

Chapter 25

Vrek

"Do you understand?" Captain hisses in my face.

He grabs my collar, yanking me off the floor; he is slightly taller than me, but I'm too tired to stand on my own.

I nod. I fight to calm my breath, but it is hard to keep it steady. Other than Captain, a few others are also around. They are here to assist with the whipping or whatever the captain wants to do.

This time, Captain didn't whip me, but maybe he hadn't gotten to that.

He hisses. "You are here to fight. Do you still remember that?"

"Yes, I said I do."

"Mind your words."

I hate this. I've been doing well and contributing. I even found us, Serena who makes us amazing food. Yet, Captain still thinks it isn't enough and he still demands more.

I can't help how I feel for her. I like her and I want her as my mate. I haven't told her yet and I'm sure as hell not going to tell Captain about that. It could be perfectly fine. She could keep making food and I could be with her. There's no need for all these punishments. Captain just needs to feel good about himself.

He watches me for another moment before he drops me on the floor. It hurts, but not that badly.

He says, "Be careful when you're around that female. She is here to work for us and not here for you to enjoy."

"Yes, I understand." Except... He can't stop how I feel for her, and I won't give up.

"Good. Now, you come with me and fix the dough-nuts."

Huh?

He heads to the door and gestures for me to follow. I don't understand what he is talking about, but at the same time, if this is a chance to get out of here, I'm going to grab it.

I push against the floor. It hurts to stand. It hurts even more to even take a breath. My lungs hurt, maybe from the whipping or just... I pat my stomach as I hold onto the wall and inch my way out of the room.

My stomach is empty. The doughnut from a while ago is still tasty in my mind, but I need more.

The other uzains walk out of the room, following me. They must be there to make sure I'm heading where the captain wants me to. Their faces are steel and show nothing.

Crazy how these are the fellows I work and fight alongside. But if I were them, I wouldn't dare to do anything either.

Maybe Captain has a point when he said Serena is a bad influence. She makes me do risky things.

I fought the Captain for her, and I would never regret that. I would do everything for my mate, even though she has no idea yet.

We arrive at the kitchen. Captain taps his fingers on the door. Is he knocking? Is he someone who will even knock?

"Come in." Serena's voice comes from the inside.

My heart pulses at that. I want her and I want her now. I bite my tongue, fighting to make sure I don't rush over and piss Captain off right here.

Captain waits. Maybe he thinks that Serena is going to open the door and come out. I would much rather go in myself so we can skip this nonsense. Serena told us to come inside, not that she was coming out. Maybe Captain should read a sign, or actually listen.

Eventually, the Captain presses the button for the door and goes in.

Inside, Serena is measuring out the ingredients, looking peaceful and intact. She pours the milk from the measuring cup into the mixing bowl. "Yes? The doughnuts won't be ready..." She sucks in a breath with her eyes snapping wide open when she sees me.

Captain clears his throat. "Is this what will fix the doughnuts?"

Huh? Is this what he mentioned earlier? That putting me here again will fix it? Were there issues with the doughnuts?

Serena comes over and she eyes me up and down. "Well, it looks like... He doesn't seem as fine as I remember."

Captain clears his throat again. "Enough is enough. Don't keep pushing."

So... Maybe this is the reason I'm safe again. Serena tried to rescue me.

Fuck... Now, I must be the most useless male ever. I can't protect her and I can't save myself either. All I can do is sit there and wait for her to save me.

Captain shrugs. "Now that you know he is still alive, you can start giving me the good doughnuts."

Serena nods. "Yes, I will. Don't worry about that. You know I've been doing what I was told."

Captain nods, but there is a half-scowl on his face. Maybe he thinks that Serena and I are together, which he hates. He leaves without saying another word, which may or may not be good news.

When the door is securely closed, Serena goes over to the window and checks the piece of paper there. Looks like there have been changes since. She is reinforcing the no-peeking rule even harder.

She lets out a breath, standing against the door. "Good to know you're still alive."

"You bet. I thought you hated me."

"I do. You are a bad uzain." She looks away from me, but I know she cares about me. If she doesn't, she won't help me... Wait!

I wrap my arms around her and grab her to my chest. Her soft body presses against me, making blood rush through my whole body. "I'm a bad uzain, and a pretty useless one. I hate how I can't protect you."

She hugs me back and strokes my back. "I hope you are fine. Thank you for trying to help me."

"Did Captain do anything to you? When you... I mean, you smelled like him for a bit. Are you fine?"

She blinks and sniffs, seemingly trying to catch what I'm talking about. She seems confused. Maybe humans don't have sensitive noses.

"Nothing. I think he wanted to make sure you won't think I'm yours. Well, he told me to stay away from you, too."

"Are you sure? You can tell me. Maybe I can't fight him outright, but I can try to help."

"He didn't hurt me. I kept arguing with him, and he seemed to get annoyed. Left me in his room. So, instead of staying on the floor, I just slept on his bed through the night."

"Are you sure he left you there in his room but he left?"

"Yeah, but he put me into another room the next day and I'm supposed to be staying there now."

What? I hate that. I found Serena and I brought her here, so she should stay with me.

She pats my chest. "Chill. Don't think I'm yours just because I helped you. You are still a kidnapper."

I hold her cheeks. "I think I'm feeling a lot more for you than... I imagined."

She stares at me again. I think something similar happened when I told her about it earlier too. I don't want to miss this chance again.

I lean closer to her. "Serena, I know you may not think this way, but I feel something for you and that's more than just... wanting to fuck you."

She remains quiet, watching me with wide eyes.

My heart races so hard that it is tempting to shut up. Maybe that will be a bit easier. "Serena, I mean it. I know I kidnapped you, but... I want to be with you. I know Captain won't like it, but I don't want to care about that anymore. I know I'm a bad uzain to you and I'm not arguing about that. You don't need to make a decision right now either, I just want... It would be great if you gave me a chance."

She still stares at me as if she is busy thinking about that.

I shiver. I know she gets to decide for herself, but I hate how she hasn't agreed already. Maybe I'm a bit too useless and that's why she doesn't want me.

Eventually, she asks, "Why? I don't understand. Though maybe I shouldn't be surprised when you seemed to think I was yours since we met."

"I want you to be mine. I don't know the reason, but it feels that way. I've never felt that with anyone else."

She stares at me for another moment when the broadcast sounds. I hate the mechanical voice that warps whoever's actual voice. "Calling all warriors, other than the essential crew: gather for the attack."

Fuck... This is such bad timing, so bad that it almost feels like Captain is eavesdropping on us and wants to cut my conversation with Serena short.

She gasp. "What does that mean?"

"The fleet is about to land and strike. I have to go and get ready for combat."

"So... You'll be robbing someone."

I close my eyes. "You can take it that way. I'll explain more if I get to."

"Huh?"

Maybe she has never fought. "It is going to be a fight. I never know whether I'll make it back."

Her eyes widen at me. I peck a kiss on her lips. She still seems to be frozen in her spot. I pat her head again.

"I'll fight to get back here. Have some doughnuts ready for me."

She says nothing and still seems to be in shock. I would love to stay with her, but I have to go. I turn to the door and leave the kitchen.

Maybe if I fight hard and bring back the best loot, she will consider me. Who isn't looking for a strong mate to protect them, after all?

Chapter 26

Serena

Even after Vrek leaves, I remain standing in my spot. I can't move a single step. The kitchen seems to get a lot larger at once and I'm alone.

I don't know what I should be thinking about. He said he wanted me as his mate. He also said he is going off to fight, and that... he may not be able to come back if the fight turns out ugly.

He... might die...

I gasp at that. While I'm not sure whether I want him as my mate, I don't want him to die.

But... What do I do now?

Are they going to fight and leave me here in the kitchen?

Wait... If they are attacking someone, there is a chance that they are landing on some kind of planet. And for there to be things for them to raid, there have to be beings living there and maybe they will help me. At least I might be able to get out of this stupid spaceship.

My heart skips a beat. That would mean that I'd never see Vrek again.

I grit my teeth and shake my head, trying to shake the stupid thought out of my head. He may want me as his mate, but it doesn't mean I have to care about that. I have my own life to deal with and he already sent me on a tangent. I'm more than justified to hate him.

It is more important to get out of here.

I reach my hand to the button for the door when there are rapid thundering noises of boots slamming at the ground. I flinch and barely manage to take my hand back. Are they coming for me?

The boots soon go past the kitchen and keep going. Maybe they are heading to fight the poor beings on the planet.

There is no way they will come after me since I haven't even started fleeing. And when they get busy, they won't have the time to care about me. I wait until the sound of the boots is gone before I press the button and leave the kitchen.

Wait...

While I'm not a good fighter at all, maybe I should grab a knife with me, just in case.

I go back and pull one before I continue with my plan with the knife hidden.

It is quiet in the corridor. Seems like everyone is either out fighting or in the control panel getting ready for whatever can happen.

I look both ways. No one is looking at me. Maybe I should go down where the uzains went earlier.

All along the way, it is too quiet to my liking. I turn the corner and arrive at a window. There is a village outside with the Empire's flags on the fence, but that doesn't seem to be stopping the uzains anytime soon.

There is smoke from the village; maybe that's from the attack. I shiver at that. It must be a rough fight. I wish Vrek and Zil all the best if they are there fighting, but I don't have time to care about them.

I continue down the corridor, but at the other corner, I almost run into someone. I halt right before I will run into them.

"Whoa!" It is Zil and he soon frowns when he sees me. "What are you doing here?"

"Um... Trying to figure out what is happening?"

He tilts his head to the side. "We are attacking. No worries, we will take off when we get the loot. Are you lost?"

There's no way I will let him bring me back to the kitchen or "my room." "I'm fine. I'm heading to the storage unit."

"Oh, are the ingredients used up? I can help you with that."

I don't need him to follow me around. He isn't going to allow me to get out of here. "It is fine. I'm just checking the amount and making sure we get them restocked later. Maybe you should be on your duty since a lot of uzains are fighting now."

He shrugs. "Sure, just let me know if you need anything." He checks his watch and hurries down the corridor. "I'll catch you later."

Oh... Catch me later? Best of luck to him.

I hurry down the corridor too. Others won't be as easy to fool. I take a breath. There is scent of smoke and from something burning. Does that mean I'm getting close?

The door of the spaceship is opened and there's no one around. I suppose there are going to be cameras watching there so the ones on the ship will know if someone tries to attack the ship.

From where I stand, I can barely see the ground outside and it is dark out there.

Before I convince myself otherwise and lose my chance, I run down the slope almost stumbling when I'm in such a hurry that my legs seem weaker than I remember.

The village in front of me is burning. The entrance of the fence is... It looks like a monster stomped onto it and it fell apart on the floor, doing nothing meaningful.

There are shouts inside the village and that's not where I'll be going. I keep running away from the village, where the uzains are probably watching. They may see me running out of the spaceship and try to catch me again.

Far from the village, there is a forest. Maybe I should hide there until the uzains leave. The villagers should be able to help, given they aren't all dead by then.

A loud alarm sounds from the inside of the spaceship and there are specs of shadows in the sky, which... Don't look good at all.

Chapter 27

Vrek

My battle squad stomps on our enemies. The ground under my boots trembles as we tear through the villagers' defenses, which are almost non-existent. Maybe they have never been attacked before, or the Empire isn't paying them enough to fight us.

I swing my battleaxe at the soldier who dares to lift his weapon at me, chopping off his head before he can fight me. "There, the storage."

There are a few villagers there who are in the Empire's uniforms. They are sneakily still around the storage unit. I doubt they are too scared to flee.

We run down facility after facility. After we leave, it will take the Empire a lot to rebuild this place. We are going to do whatever it takes to slow them down in their plan to dominate every inch of the universe. At the same time, mass destruction here will please whoever hired us to be here.

Fights always set my blood on fire in a good way. This time, it also means I may get to please Serena and prove to her that I'm a very capable male.

We are at a crossroads and there may be others coming to attack us. The leader of my attack squad hisses for two of us to head over to the storage while the rest of us guard against the other road. "Be careful."

I run over with another on the squad. I'm going to chop their heads off. They should know the consequences of working for the Empire.

When we are steps away from them, they seem to put down something and they run to different sides. My stomach twitches for some reason.

I growl, "Retreat, uzains! Shield!" Maybe I catch a scent of something in the air, but when things are already burning, I'm not sure. But it is always better safe than sorry.

We lift the shields that are tied to our arms, right in time. There is a loud explosion.

Fuck!

It feels like the ground shifts from the power of the explosive. A sharp pain jabs through my body as I stumble backward. My organs and my horns hurt and a scent of blood spreads in my mouth.

Am I dead?

But I don't want to be dead...

When I open my eyes again, my whole body is screaming in pain. I gasp and it hurts. But I can breathe.

Someone runs over to me. "Talk to me!"

"Not dead." I barely make out the words. My whole body is heating up but without more pain. I force my eyes wider to see Luz, one of my squad, using a healing ray gun on me.

The other who ran to the storage unit with me is moaning in pain by my side.

At least we aren't dead.

"Hold tight for me." Luz squeezes my arm.

I open my mouth to ask when he pats me and says, "Yes, I already called the other squads."

The explosion must be the Empire's attempt to destroy what's in the storage, which means my squad probably has found the right place: where they keep their weapons. This has to be more important than the food storage we found earlier.

There are more uzains running over to help, alongside transport ships that will take our loot back to the main ship. But one of them points at the sky.

I glance and the captain's voice comes from the earbud, which all of us on the battlefield have.

"Uzains, get everything we can and retreat. The Empire is coming. Board the battleships."

Fuck... How did they come around this quickly?

At least my squad alone has moved a lot of grain, not to mention the other attacking squads. This will be a successful attack regardless.

Luz helps me up. I gasp from the pain and force myself to move. Uzains help one another, but I will hate myself forever if I slow down Luz and cause him trouble.

A few come over and help me. This isn't how I wanted to look in front of Serena, but this is still better than getting killed or tortured to death if I ended up in the Empire's hands. No matter how mad Captain would be when he knew about Serena and me, he wouldn't kill me. Yet, the Empire would want me to be dead for sure.

The shadows above us get bigger and bigger. We can only hope the Empire's reinforcement isn't that strong.

Our main ship is already in the air, getting ready to fight.

My squad's battleship is now in sight. The pain in me grows and every breath hurts more, but... I have to keep going.

Serena... Are you waiting for me?

Chapter 28

Serena

This planet is a cold place. I hide inside the thick forest, but I can't help but peek out of a thick tree in the direction of the village.

The poor place is burning. Even though I'm a safe distance away, the smoke lingers.

I shiver when there is a loud bang from the village. Is that... an explosion?

I gasp and my blood seems to chill. Vrek...

Fuck this! I'm not supposed to be worried about him. He chose to raid the village, and if something happens to him, that's what he chose too.

I clench onto the rough tree bark; it hurts, but the load in my chest is worse. My throat is so tight that it feels like I can't breathe.

What if Vrek dies?

I grit my teeth when blood seems to drain out of my head. There is no reason I have to care this much about him, but... I shiver and it feels like I'm the one injured or hurt.

I'm about to turn away and go deeper into the woods when there is another loud bang.

There are spaceships flying and they are firing at each other. I suppose the village got reinforcements from somewhere.

Is Vrek on one of the spaceships?

The big spaceship I fled from isn't there anymore, so maybe it is also in the air, fighting.

I should go deeper into the forest just to make sure I won't get hit. But at the same time...

Just standing here and watching isn't going to change anything for the uzains. It isn't like I know whether I want Vrek to be fine, either. He never explained clearly what his fleet does.

There are sparks in the sky and things falling to the ground. I close my eyes with my heart hurting. What if Vrek is dead?

I don't know why I have to care, but I can't make myself forget about him.

It feels like I can't breathe and I hate that. I sit on the ground and lean against the tree, gasping. What should I do?

The trees offer me their canopy and those fighting out there probably won't have the time to come chasing behind me. Whoever is reinforcing the village won't know about me; the uzains probably won't risk staying here for longer than they need to.

I'm... safe?

This is what I've been fighting to do. I'm out of the uzains' ship and those kidnappers won't be able to get me.

I should be happy, but at the same time...

Fuck...

Tears roll down my cheeks. I can't even control them.

Vrek... I miss him. I don't know why, but maybe he means a bit more to me than I want to admit.

Other than kidnapping me, maybe he has been trying to treat me well. It's just...

I shake my head and force myself to stand. I'm getting out of that stupid place and I'm going to start a life of my own again. If there is a village over there, there have to be others living here, and some of them could help me, for sure.

I run into the forest, making sure the knife is still with me. First, survive the night...

Chapter 29

Vrek

It feels like my body is falling apart. They put me on the healing ray machine and I fight to keep my eyes closed as the ray works on me. At the same time, I have to stay awake, so the vibration from the ray won't over-stimulate my body.

But... When I got back to the ship, the fight was still going on. My squad got to retreat to the base ship earlier because of the two of us getting badly injured. I suppose the other injured uzain is in the device to the side of me.

I hate to be the reason we wasted time. The Empire's reinforcement should die with the village that serves them.

Pain surges through me as the machine buzzes. This is what I warned Serena about. If she keeps fighting us, we can beat her up, shove her into the machine, and beat her up again.

Heat surges as the healing ray echoes through my body. It hurts so badly that I'd rather remain injured outside. But at the same time, this is the treatment I need. The heat and pain are here now, but they won't last.

I clench a fist, swallowing with my throat that is so dry that it feels like I've swallowed too many bread with water.

Fuck...

Worse, when I was back on the spaceship, I didn't see Serena. She knew I went out.

But maybe she didn't know I came back.

When the pain is finally over and the machine hisses as the cover is lifted, the spaceship shudders.

Did we get hit?

"Fuck..." Someone swears and there are thumping sounds nearby. Maybe whoever is here to check me out stumbled.

"What happened?" My throat still hurts, but the pain has mostly subsided.

The healer is here and it's good to see him. He says, "I don't know. I'm here with you. We are fighting the reinforcements to the storage village, that's all I know."

"Okay..." I take a breath when my heart rate is spiking again. "Tell me, where's Serena?"

He shakes his head. "I'm not sure. It is busy during the fight and I haven't looked for her."

That's reasonable, but doesn't help with my racing heart. "I get it. How am I?"

"Okay, looking from the report—"

I lift a hand to stop him. "Cut to the chase. Please? I want to help and fight. So, in short, do I get to leave?" I have to see Serena for myself to believe that she is fine. My heart is in the air and I need her.

"Well, you aren't at your peak, but you can move around."

I hop off the machine before he can come over to help. That's all I needed to know. "Thanks."

I hurry out of the door with him sighing behind my back. I don't have time for that. I head to the control panel when I almost bump into Zil.

The scowl on his face is... I ask, "What happened?"

"Did you see Serena?"

I shake my head. "I was just out of the healing zone. What happened?"

"I... I don't know. I can't find her anywhere. She said she was going to check the storage area, but then... I have no idea where she is. I meant to check on the doughnuts, but she isn't in the kitchen."

"What?" I growl, but soon sigh. "Sorry, I don't mean to be rude. Are you sure she's missing?"

"I don't know. She might be hiding. I mean, she might be scared of the fight."

I frown at that. Maybe she's never been caught in a fight before, but I don't think she's such a timid being. "I'll find her."

"Okay, I'll try too. The doughnuts were too good to miss."

I want the doughnuts, but I want her too. And she is more important than what she can get me. I need her to stay sane.

Dashing down the corridor, I glance at the window. The fight is still going on. There are the Empire's space-ships flying outside with laser ray guns firing at us. We fire back and... I don't have the luxury to be standing at the window and watching the fight.

I turn a corner, arriving at the stairs to the battleship port. The captain is coming up the stairs. I take a step back and bow my head.

He comes around and nods. "Vrek, glad to know you made it."

So... He knows about the explosion. "Thank you. By the way, have you seen Serena?"

He pauses and doesn't give me the answer, which should be simple.

"Vrek."

"Yes?"

"You understand we have to prioritize the fight and the fleet, right?"

I suck in a breath. This doesn't sound good at all. But we are uzains, so it will be impossible for us to give Serena to the Empire for whatever reasons. "I do. Once I'm got of the healing machine, I came and try to help."

He nods. "I know you can be good at that. When we were still on the planet fighting, she fled."

"What?" My eyes widen and my brain goes blank. "She what?"

"She fled the ship. We didn't have enough uzains to catch her."

I lean onto the wall before I stumble and fall to the ground. "She... what?"

"I said she fled the spaceship and I have no idea where she went."

Fuck...

How is that even possible? I thought she was fine staying here with us. And I told her to stay here and I would be back.

Or...

Maybe she has been wanting to leave and found a chance...

But this is a uzain spaceship, so there's no way she could flee with no one knowing. Unless...

I glare at Captain, who has an annoying blank face that shows absolutely nothing other than how he doesn't even care about that. I straighten. "I'll look for her."

"We are fighting the Empire. There's no time to look for her."

I open my mouth, but I can't make a word come out. I know he is right, but at the same time, I can't just let her go. I didn't even have a chance to say goodbye. Maybe she really wanted to leave, but...

Captain scowls at me. "What's on your mind?"

"Nothing."

"Don't lie."

"I have to find her."

"We can survive without doughnuts."

"She means more to me than that. Please... let me look for her."

"The base ship will stay to fight. I have to."

"I know. I don't expect the base ship to go with me. Can I have a battleship? Or maybe just a transport ship? Please?"

Whether he agrees or not, I'm going to do something.

Captain lifts his brows at me. "She fled."

"I'll talk to her."

"Why bother? We can look for another being who can make us doughnuts."

I look away from him, fighting to say nothing.

He watches me and doesn't seem to be giving up his question either. But the longer we stand here doing the dumb staring game, the further away Serena could go. That's not a safe planet for her. I have to get her out of there. Even if she doesn't want to stay here, she should go to a safer place.

I'm about to go down the stairs and ignore Captain's glare when he shrugs and says, "You can take a transport ship. All the battleships are out fighting."

"Thanks!" I slide to his side and hurry down the stairs.

"Be careful. You may have to manage to get off the planet yourself before we can pick you up."

"I will."

As soon as I reach the transport ship, I jump into it and start it.

I have to get going. Serena...

I just have to make it through the battlefield, and reach the surface of the planet without crashing. It has to be easy... unless it's not.

Chapter 30

Serena

The deeper I go into the forest, the quieter it is. The fighting is distant, but in my heart, the firing of laser beams and fire are still going on.

I have to forget about those crazy uzains.

The forest gets darker and darker. I almost can't even see my fingers when I spread out my arm to the fullest.

Leaves rustle under my feet. I'm not fit for walking in the forest, especially in the darkness.

I turn around and stare at the sky, but the canopy is too thick to see through.

Vrek is going to find out that I've left. Will he be upset about that?

My heart races again and heat surges through me. I think I miss his arms.

But I don't need that. I can be on my own.

I find a tree with rougher bark and lower branches. Before something comes and gets me, I should climb up there to be safe.

I step on the tree and hop to grab a branch when there is a shuffle in the air and it feels like the ground shakes.

What happened?

Maybe that means I should climb quicker.

I'm almost at a thick enough branch when my hand touches something slimy, which is definitely not a branch and not a leaf.

It growls and I let go of the thing. Instead of climbing down the tree, I fall off it.

But I don't even have time to yelp before something lands on the ground next to me.

I start off running. I don't even know where I'm heading, I just have to keep going.

It is too dark to even know what is chasing behind me. All I know is I interrupted its sleep and it isn't happy with me.

There is a growl from the beast. I weave through the trees, trying my best to make it hard for the beast to catch me.

Where is Vrek? He can save me, right?

I still have my knife with me, but I'm not going to win against that beast.

I take another turn when the tree I'm going around shudders and snaps.

The four-legged beast that looks like a leopard with horns and two tails glares at me. I'm tiny in front of it and won't even be enough for its dinner.

I brandish my knife at it, but it huffs, not even caring about that.

With that huge paw, he could snap me into half easier than he did with the tree.

The beast leaps and he crashes over onto me. I lift the knife to stab it, but its paw hits the knife out of my hand.

Its hot breath lands on my throat when I kick its stomach and punch its nose. It growls and bites at my poor arm.

I didn't run away from the uzains just to become this beast's dinner!

Maybe staying with Vrek wasn't that bad.

Fuck!

There is another growl and a scent of burned fur.

The beast jumps and snarls. But before it can bite at me again, something smashes at the beast and it stumbles to the side.

I roll around at once, even though it feels like I may have died.

There are the bright beams of laser guns and the beast hisses. But eventually, it disappears into the forest. Gone without a trace.

I remain on the ground, my whole body too exhausted to move.

"How are you doing?" Whoever saved me comes over. I can only hope they aren't here to eat me instead.

"Serena?"

Huh? Do I know them? It is so dark here. Or maybe I've been so nervous that my brain can't process a single thing.

A pair of arms grab my shoulders and shake me. "Serena, hey! I'm Vrek."

"Vrek?"

"Yes! I missed you." He wraps me into his arms and our bodies press against each other. His warm chest is better than anything else I've felt.

He holds me tighter and tighter to his chest as if he is trying to squeeze me flat. "I missed you. Why did you leave without a word? Do you hate me? Do you not want to stay on the spaceship? I—"

"Beast... Village..." Fuck... I can't even talk now. What's wrong with me?

I gasp, trying to regain my calm, but I can't. My brain is still screaming and I have no idea what I should do or say.

He strokes my back. "It's okay. You are safe now. We will talk later."

"Back to the ship."

"Yes. it will be better than being here when..." He looks around. "Let's go. We are winning against the Empire, for now, so we should leave before they regroup."

So... After trying so hard to leave, I'm heading back there. After I fled, they will be watching me and make sure I never have a chance again.

I look away when Vrek sighs. "Serena... You hate me, right? And you don't want to go back there with me."

"Thanks for saving me."

"I..." He sighs. "Please, I can let you go, but don't stay here, okay? It is dangerous."

I close my eyes with tears swelling in me. "Captain..."

"I'll talk to him. I'll make sure you get out of there safely." There is a painful frown on his face, which also hurts me.

The heat inside me is back and when he holds me this tightly, my heart beats for him, even though I hate that. "Vrek... You win..."

"It's not about winning or losing." He groans, his voice filled with pain. "I have to take you back with me. I'm sorry, but I can't let you be out here in danger."

He gathers me in his arms and starts walking. I'm too tired to fight him. I don't know what I want. He isn't wrong. I don't want to become some beast's dinner, but at the same time... What will be waiting for me?

This is the second time Vrek saved me when he didn't have to... Fuck, when will I stop owing him?

Chapter 31

Vrek

"Serena..." I sit on the bed next to her. Captain said she must stay in her room, but there are no rules making me stay in mine. I don't even care about what he thinks. I have to take care of her.

The tray with food is on the chair right next to her, waiting for her, but she doesn't seem to be interested.

I know she hates the bread we have here, so I get her bacon and eggs, but she still doesn't seem to care.

I've tried all kinds of food with her, but she has eaten nothing since I brought her back to the spaceship.

It hurts to watch her emotionless face, which probably means that she hates me. Maybe she figured that I'm not worth arguing with or even talking to.

I sigh. "Eat something, okay? You can't keep doing this. It's been days, and you haven't eaten a single thing or even drunk something. Or do you not want to see me? I can leave."

Except I've left her alone a lot of times already, she still never touches her food.

I sigh again, that's the only thing I can manage. "Please talk to me? I know I annoy you, but... please?"

She watches me with those calm but cold eyes. Has she given up on surviving?

I climb onto the bed, but she has taken the center spot and doesn't move a tiny bit. I wrap my arms around her. "I mean it. I'll arrange somewhere for you to go. It is okay if you don't want to stay here. It's... I'm sorry if I... It's just... When I feel you and understand that you may just be the mate I've been looking for, I couldn't stop myself."

I pat her side. "Hey, at least you didn't become the beast's dinner. And we can eat some meat instead."

She moves slightly but still looks away from me.

I lean closer. She doesn't move away. I hope that's not because she has given up. "Serena, I wanted a chance for us. But I understand if you don't want it." Fuck... This hurts a lot more than it sounded in my head. "I'll always miss you, but I hope the best for you too, doing what you want."

It feels like she grabbed my heart and tore it out of my chest. But... It is miserable how she doesn't feel anything for me, nothing but hate.

She sighs when her stomach rumbles. I'm about to ask again when she says, "Just like that? Are you really going to put me on another planet?"

"Yes, somewhere far away from the Empire if that's what you want. Or back to your cafe. I'll make sure you arrive there safely."

"So... You don't want doughnuts anymore?"

Oh... That will suck. I love the doughnuts, and every uzain does, too. "No, I don't want those. I want you to be happy instead."

She turns around, facing me with her sad face. I grit my teeth. My horns feel out of place in front of her and I hate every moment of this. I lean my horn to her, wanting a stroke from her. She watches me, but her hands don't move a single inch.

I say, "Please? I'm sorry."

"I'm tired."

I let go of her and keep my distance. "Sorry."

She shakes her head and sits up. She pulls the tray over and starts eating.

All I can do is stare at her.

At least she is eating, so this means things are getting better, right?

Serena

I chew the bacon as my stomach grumbles and moans. Maybe I should have eaten something long ago. I wasn't trying to complain to Vrek by not eating and drinking. I just... couldn't figure out what to do and what to think. And... Maybe that's the reason I didn't want food.

Vrek is watching me. It seems like he is trying not to breathe, as if he may interrupt me and I will stop eating again.

Now... that gaze is sending shivers down my spine. "Why are you staring at me like this?"

He blinks. "Well, I'm happy you are eating now."

"Yeah, I'm hungry."

"Oh... You weren't hungry or thirsty?"

"Yes, I was. I don't understand either, so don't ask."

His mouth opens and closes and he looks like a balloon that is so full that it may pop.

I shrug. "I'm glad you didn't bring me the stringy bread."

He wraps his arms around me. "I worry about you. When I found you in the forest, I ran faster than I probably could ever do again."

"Right, I haven't thanked you." I run my hand along his chest. There is... a mark on his arm that's not the black swirl on the other parts of his body. "Did you... Fuck..." I reach my finger at that and he flinches. I stop, not touching that when it looks like it hurts.

He smiles with pride. "It doesn't hurt a lot. I smacked the beast with my battleaxe."

"You used a laser gun."

"Oh! That too."

"Caught you." I can't help but grin. He makes me happy. "Trying to look strong, huh?"

"You know I'm strong."

Maybe it isn't that bad to be here with him again. "How did... the fight go?"

His eyes narrow on me. "Well, it went great. We smacked the Empire's ass and took all their weapons."

I suppose I'm not against that. He watches me for another moment as if he is trying to make sure I'm fine with that. He continues, "And we took their food and supplies. Also made them blow up their storage units."

Wait...! "What was that village?"

"From what the captain told us, that's a place where the Empire hides their stuff. We were hired to take everything or destroy everything."

"Someone hired the fleet?"

"Yes, and they are going to pay us handsomely." As he says that, his face falls. "And... we are going to land in a space station to unload the stuff we got from the Empire."

"Do you not like space stations?"

He glances to the side. "I like them. There are interesting things there, a lot better than staying on the ship. And that will mean the fleet is going to have a short break from flying."

I suppose we are heading to the Alliance, the Empire's sworn enemy in the galaxy, or at least somewhere that's neutral.

I ask, "Then why are you upset?"

He takes a deep breath. "I know you've been wanting to leave. So... I'll give you my allowance when we arrive there. You can catch a spaceship to go home."

Oh... My eyes widen and... tears surge in my eyes.

He squeezes out a smile and gets out of the bed. "Yeah, I just want you to be happy. Don't tell anyone, though. I'm not supposed to."

He heads to the door and I'm not sure whether I should follow him. He says, "I mean, even if you are to flee, I want you to at least go somewhere safe."

He leaves without looking back, but his sad face when he told me about that cut deep.

I'm alone again. And... very soon, I'll... be all alone again at home.

That's what I've wanted. But when it's happening so soon...

I close my eyes, and how the beast chased me comes into mind again. He should have been fighting with his team, but somehow, he showed up and saved me.

Even before I was chased, I missed Vrek. Now... the thought of him sends warmth to me. And... the thought of never seeing him again somehow pains me. There are twitches on my arms as if something is pulsing inside me. I don't understand Vrek... He is confusing...

Chapter 32

Serena

I put the ingredients into the mixing bowl and glance up at the door. I hope no one will come here. I've told all the uzains to leave me alone and to not even line up.

The window on the door is blocked. So... I won't even know whether someone is out there.

I take a breath and start mixing the ingredients together. Maybe I need to do something so I won't sink too deeply into my own thoughts.

The doughnuts I'm making are the reason I'm here. But maybe there are more reasons for that.

I want to run into Vrek and enjoy him here and there. Maybe he is just a big guy who is bad at expressing himself.

He didn't have to be there in the forest when I fled from the spaceship, clearly showing him that I didn't want to be here.

The captain won't be happy about that. The uzains are probably rigid with how the fleet should fight and no one should be doing their own thing.

Did the Captain know about that?

There is a knock on the door. I thought I'd already posted a note on the door. "I'm busy. Go away."

"Are you sure this is how you talk to me, human?"

Fuck... It is the captain...

"But I'm making doughnuts."

"Stop making those for a bit."

Yeah... That's *so obvious.* But it isn't like he is going to care. "Fine, come in."

The door slides open and the captain lifts his brows at me. "What happened to you?"

"Huh?"

He taps my forehead as if I have a button on my forehead or something. "This isn't going to produce good doughnuts."

"You don't know a thing about doughnuts."

He shrugs. "I don't care. I think you are the reason Vrek is wandering around with his soul elsewhere. What are you going to do about that?"

"What do you mean?"

He lifts his brows. "I told you not to mess around with me. Vrek is supposed to be here fighting instead of getting distracted. I thought I was clear about that."

"That's not my problem."

"He was injured in the fight, but he rushed to look for you when he knew you fled. I couldn't change his mind."

"What?" I bite my tongue, trying to stop myself from asking for more information. Was Vrek injured? And he still had to fight the beast to save me? "What happened to him?"

"Well, his team ran into the explosives and he was one of the ones in the front."

My eyes snap wide open. Given that Vrek is here, and I just talked to him, he isn't dead, but... "And? What happened next?"

"The Empire's sneaky minions destroyed their own storage, so we couldn't take the things inside. The fleet took him back. He was injured, but not too badly. Then... his silly ass ran off to save you once he knew you fled."

"When he was injured?"

"We used the healing ray on him. I told him to just let you go when we were busy fighting the Empire's reinforcements."

"So... You knew I fled."

"I do. I watched you running out of the spaceship with the security camera. I'm not blind."

Fuck... But I'm not surprised. I shrug. "You could have stopped me."

"I could. But I didn't want to waste my time and my fleet's effort in chasing your heels. If you want to be on the worst planet ever, feel free to die."

I shiver at that. Although I fight to hide it, he smirks. I scowl at that. "You must be mad. I'm not dead."

"I'm mad. Vrek became a soulless being because of you."

"You hoped I'd die."

"No, I don't. I don't care whether you are dead or not. You were the one running out of my ship. If you were dead, it was by your choice, not mine. I didn't kill you and I didn't kick you off the ship."

I fold my arms. "Whatever. Why are you here?"

Vrek came to me when he should be resting and healing. Yet... And he offered for me to leave on the space station.

Captain clears his throat and yanks my mind back to him. "What's on your mind?"

"Why should I tell you?"

"I thought you knew better. Do we have to try that again?"

For him to smack my head to the wall? No, I don't want that. "I was asking, what are you here for? To make me feel sorry for Vrek?"

He leans closer and says, "Oh, you will feel sorry for yourself soon."

What?

I take half a step back when he closes the distance at once. I hiss at him, fighting to look braver than I am. "What are you planning?"

"That's my question to you. You tried to flee. Did you think there'd be no consequences for that? Not to mention, when Vrek insisted on driving a transport ship to look for you, he could have died. I didn't have enough ships to help him to even stand a chance."

"I don't understand where you are heading."

"Tell me, are you going to stay here or are you going to keep fleeing and hurting Vrek? He is a great warrior, and I don't want him to end up a mushy pile of mess."

Huh? "I thought you hated how he seems to care about me."

"Yes. I'm not changing my mind, but you should stop messing with my warrior. Are you going to stay or not? I can't have him running places trying to rescue you. Look at you: he came back with you with a scratch on his arm and you are intact."

I stare at him. I... I don't know what I want when I somehow can choose. More importantly... "I don't want to cause him issues. You aren't going to like it if I'm here. Maybe all you want is doughnuts."

"You bet. That's the reason I even allow you to exist here. Vrek has been crazy about you."

Heat streams onto my cheeks, like my cheeks couldn't get any redder. I hate this. I don't need this now when the captain is watching me closely.

I shrug. "I have to keep going with the doughnuts or the magic won't work on them. Maybe you should leave."

"Are you telling me what to do?"

"Yes." I walk off. I don't want to talk to him. He isn't threatening to kill me, but at the same time, it feels off.

He comes behind me. "You are lucky I'm an honorable male. Otherwise, a lot worse things could happen to you. And if all I care about is my own pleasure..."

I spin around and glare at him. "Are you threatening to do something to me?"

"No, I won't. I'm just thinking. I've never seen Vrek that crazy for someone. He has been a great warrior. When he said he found someone to make us doughnuts, this isn't what I expected."

"Like... I'd be just a slave working on the doughnuts?"

He muses. "Maybe." He heads to the door. "When the doughnuts are ready, I will have one. I'm the captain, so..."

"You won't line up and wait."

He laughs. "Maybe I know why everyone kind of likes you now."

He leaves, and I remain staring at the closed door. He said what? Everyone kind of like me? I blink at that, trying to make sure I heard him right.

Captain has never liked me. So if he said everyone kind of likes me, maybe that means everyone actually really likes me. Maybe it is for my doughnuts, but I won't hate that either.

Vrek... I miss him. But... How am I supposed to know whether he means it? Like... He mentioned that he wanted me as his mate. He risked his life to save me twice, so... Does that mean...?

And maybe that's the reason he is the only one here who can send warmth into me, even when we aren't touching each other.

And he knows how to please me...

Chapter 33

Vrek

I continue down the training field after my round of practice fights. I hate every minute of this. Maybe I shouldn't have told Serena about my plan until it was time. Now...

It is torture to be here when I would much rather be with her, spending more time with her.

But maybe she doesn't want me, so this may be better for her.

Someone elbows me and interrupts my thoughts. I hate that and I'm about to growl when I realize that it's Zil. I don't growl at Zil.

He frowns. "Are you fine? It feels like I've been asking that a lot recently. You keep running into trouble."

"As if you didn't get into some trouble yourself."

He groans. "Come on. We are not talking about that."

I shrug. "I'm as fine as I can be."

"Do the injuries still hurt?"

"No, the healing ray did well." My injuries don't hurt anymore, but my heart hurts and I can't tell him about that. He may be able to guess it, but what if others hear that? It won't be good for Serena or me.

"But your mind isn't here."

I shrug. "That's impossible. My mind is always with me."

"Except I don't think so."

He pats my shoulder before he stands in the line for his turn. Coach presses the button for the buzzer and the ones in the round dash off before they will be last and get punished.

I stare at them. I should pay attention to the run so I will be on the starting line on time and have the best shot. But it feels like I can't focus on that at all. All I can think about is Serena.

She will be happy when she gets back to her life. I think I should be happy knowing that she'll be enjoying her life. But I'll never see her again.

Ouch... Knowing she is my mate makes it hurt even more. I've asked, but she hasn't agreed. Maybe that means she isn't my mate. But I can feel it: we are meant to be together.

"Vrek, what the hell are you doing?" The coach growls at me, and I put my feet to the starting line at once. He murmurs something under his breath as he starts the buzzer.

I dash off with the others in my round. There are pillars on the ground to run around, then tall staircases to jump onto. I barely get to the top of the stack when the rings hanging from the metal bars above present themselves.

Taking a step back, I gather the momentum to hop and grab the ring, swinging my body to reach for the next.

The coach said I could stop if I needed to since he knew I was injured in the fight. I'm fine and I'm not going to use that to get out of my training.

I kick in the air to give myself the last inch I need to get to the platform on the other end.

Fuck! I land on the platform, but I'm on the edge and hanging on it with my arms. If I fall onto the ground, I will have to restart with the rings, but technically, I'm not on the floor, so...

I push and kick, barely climbing back up onto the platform. Maybe I should focus on the training instead of thinking about Serena.

Now, I'm behind others who are already at the pool. There are floating blocks in the pool, and at the other side, there's the bell to tap as the goalpost.

A few fall into the water and swim back to where I'm standing to restart their run.

I hop to the first one, then the next, trying to keep my footing as the blocks shift and wobble. I keep going, but the uzain in front of me messes up and ends up in the water with a splash. I wince at the water, but then I slip at the next block, also ending up in the water.

Fuck this stupid thing...

I'm about to swim back to the starting point when everyone stops. I look around... The captain is here. Fuck...

He doesn't care about training sessions most of the time. Coach is the one doing it and Captain trusts him completely. Coach is also great at training us. Why is Captain here?

Captain and Coach talks and Coach gestures for me to get out of the pool. I swim over to the edge of the pool, kicking against the water to get out of it. "Captain."

He gives me a nod with his steel-hard face. He heads to the door, so I hurry to follow. What's wrong?

When we are outside of the training area, he turns around. "How's your training?"

"Um... Good?"

"I've heard you've been distracted and pretty much a slacker lately."

I swallow. Is that why he is here? But I thought performance-related issues were also dealt with by Coach. "I've been trying my best."

Wait... is this about Serena? Captain did say that if she is distracting, I'd suffer the consequences. I grit my teeth. It won't be long before I let her go, so... I hope nothing big is going to happen and stop my plan.

He folds his arms and eyes me up and down. "Where is she?"

"I suppose she is in her room? Or if she is feeling better, maybe in the kitchen. I think she is startled."

"After she fled and was caught, without a single consequence?"

"Well, she was chased and almost became a beast's dinner."

"She chose that for herself."

I grit my teeth. I don't care whether she did it to herself or not; as long as it is within my zone of influence, I'm going to protect her.

Even when she doesn't want me...

Captain lifts an eyebrow at me. "So... Do you still want to keep her with you?"

I want to, but she doesn't want to. Do I tell Captain the truth? Or... What if he will do something against her wish and I'll end up hurting her by being honest about it?

I shrug. "You're the captain."

"I thought you'd forgotten about that. When I told you to leave her alone on that stupid planet, you didn't seem to remember that I was the captain."

My throat tightens and I can't make out a word. He isn't wrong, but I don't want to admit it. I'm not supposed to feel something for Serena, even though it's driving me crazy and I want to be with her already.

Captain waits for another moment as if he is trying to get a response out of me. Except I really can't give him a response that will benefit Serena. It's okay if she is leaving and I will never see her again; I just want her to be happy.

He clears his throat. "You are a male and should know what you want. We know what we want here and we take what we want. We are uzains, dammit."

What does that mean? What is he referring to?

He muses. "If I were you, I'd fight harder for what I want."

Is that... an invitation for me to keep Serena and make her my mate? But... what if she doesn't want that?

He walks off. So... what should I do?

I already told Serena that she would be able to go home. I'm a male who will take what I want, but at the same time, I'm also a male of my word.

Chapter 34

Serena

I sit on the bed after spending the whole day making doughnuts. I like it when the uzains are happy. That's the reason I have a cafe. I want to make beings happy with my doughnuts.

The wall stares at me from across. It is... boring and cold here in the room.

Vrek isn't here. I don't know where he is. Maybe he doesn't want to see me. I kept a doughnut for him, but he never showed up. I ended up giving it to another uzain. It would be better to be eaten fresh.

What is he up to? Is everything going well?

There is a twitch in my stomach and a load in my chest. I think I miss him. Do I... actually want him? To stay here with him and...to be his mate?

I pause at the door. Captain said I should stay in my own room. I can't say I hate how he gave me this room, but at the same time...

Maybe I should look for Vrek. I don't want to get him into trouble, but I can't stay here and stay in my head for that long. I press the button for the door to open.

I step out of the room, but there is a shadow and—

Before I can halt, I slam into someone. "Ouch!"

"I'm sorry!" It's Vrek. Somehow he is at my door. "Are you okay? I didn't see you and I didn't expect you to be right behind the door."

"That's what I'm meant to say. You are the one standing right at my door for some reason. What are you doing—?"

He pushes me as he looks around. "Hush, get inside first."

"Fine."

He comes in and the door closes. "Phew, what if someone sees me?"

"And? What will happen?"

"Hey, you know Captain isn't supposed to know that I've been here."

"You are so scared of him."

He huffs. "I just want to keep us away from his attention, okay?"

He pauses as he watches me. I swallow. This doesn't seem to be good. Is he here with bad news? He leans closer and lowers his voice even though no one will be able to hear us. "The ship will be arriving at the space station tomorrow."

Is he here to say goodbye?

He forces a tight smile. "Are you happy about that? You won't have to stay here for much longer."

"Sounds like you want to offload me." My heart squeezes. Is he... Maybe he isn't interested in me after all. Maybe I'm the one overthinking it.

He wraps his arms around me and holds me so close to his chest that he can choke me. "I... I mean, I just want you to be happy."

"What does that mean?"

He pulls back and watches me with wide eyes. "I thought you wanted to go back to your place."

"I do? I built the cafe and everything and it has been my life."

"I know..." He looks away.

My heart hammers in my chest. Will it be wrong if I ask to stay?

I... Maybe it isn't going to be so bad if I stay here with him. His fleet... Maybe I don't agree with everything they do, but... It is hard to say that I agree with the Empire, either.

He gives my hand a squeeze and before I know it, he lifts me and puts me on the bed. "While you are here tonight..."

"Yes, you can stay here with me."

He smiles, but it's still a sad one. He lies by my side and gathers me into his arms. His hot body warms me and I snuggle closer to him.

He sighs. "Serena, I'm happy to have you here with me, even if it is just for a short while."

"Does Captain know about this? How you plan to let me go."

"No, hell no. He would kill me."

"So... it won't end up well when I go missing."

"Maybe. But the space station is huge and there are a lot of beings. It will be impossible for him to find you again. You just have to be careful and board the right spaceship that will bring you home."

Is he... willing to take the consequence for me to be free again? Just so... I will be happy again?

"Vrek..."

"Yes?"

I pat his chest and stroke his strong muscles. He lets out a soft moan. "Serena... Be careful of your hand. I'm not that good at keeping myself in check."

I stroke him some more and my hand wander lower. "And what will happen?"

"You want my cock, huh?"

"Maybe?" I smirk at him. It would be great if I knew what was in his head. But his thick skull may be stopping it.

He grabs my shoulder and rolls to hover over me. "Look, you're just being a tease."

"Vrek... Thank you for everything you've done for me."

He grimaces but puts up a smile soon enough. "It's okay. I just want you to be happy."

"Sounds like you love me a bit too much."

He leans closer and closer until our lips meet. "Maybe I do."

Oh...

He presses his lips on me and his hands work on me. It doesn't take long before I'm naked.

"I mean it. Serena, I..."

He...?

Maybe he feels something for me? Is that what he's going to tell me?

His jaw is tight, but he says nothing else. He rubs between my legs and moans. "Fuck, you're so wet."

Ah... Maybe this is what we need, a distraction.

I wrap my arms around him and he rubs his cock against me in no time.

"Vrek... Is this what you want to tell me?"

He grunts. "Quiet, other than moans and screams."

"Deal, if you make this good." My body is burning. I want his touch, but I'm scared of what will happen after this ends.

"You know this is going to be great." He presses his tip into me. "You want me."

"Maybe I do."

He shudders and groans. "You are insufferable."

He shoves deep into me, the thick bands on his cock rubbing my wall as he goes deeper and deeper. "You know... Fuck... You're so tight."

What's on his mind? He was going to say something, but he kept stopping himself. I want to ask whether he feels something for me too. And... When he said that he wanted me as his mate, did he mean it? Or... Did he change his mind?

More importantly, do I ask him about that? Or do I...?

I shiver when he starts pounding into me. Pleasure surges through me and it soon grows so strong that I can't even think. All I can feel is him and... nothing seems to be important anymore.

"Vrek!" I scream when an orgasm explodes through me. This is so good.

I squeeze his back, trying my best to contain my moan. No one can hear me from the outside, but I don't want to give Vrek all the enjoyment. He has to work harder if he wants my moan.

"Serena... You drive me crazy." He gasps and with his breath, the markings on his body seem to have a life of their own. It has to be his muscles moving, but... Fuck... he is a pretty handsome uzain.

I wrap my legs around his waist, arching to take his huge cock better. He gives me so much pleasure and I can't stop myself from loving that. This is crazy.

The first time I let him fuck me, he was so massive that he scared me. But... He just does it for me even more now than before. If he used to worry about breaking me, now he ravishes me.

"Vrek, you are such a monster."

"And you love it."

"Fuck yes!" I scream as another wave of pleasure strikes me. My pussy squeezes hard against his huge cock, wanting even more.

He grunts and picks up speed. The intensity in his eyes burns through my soul.

His cock seems to grow thicker and harder in me, as if that's even possible. I like how me ravishes me, and he keeps impressing me even more.

He grunts. "I want more. You are so perfect for me."

"This is so good."

His cock twitches. "I'm going to fill you up. You are such a tease and should be moaning instead."

"Make me."

He growls and slams his cock into the deepest part of me. I scream from the orgasm and his cock hammers into me, spilling his hot cum. "Serena... I've warned you enough times."

"Fuck!" I scream even more and I'm milking him so hard that he grunts.

He shudders and fills me up even more before he rolls to the side and pulls out of me. "Serena... I'll miss you."

I snuggle up to him and he strokes my hair. Maybe this is what it is. Tomorrow, I will be on a spaceship heading home and he will be in this spaceship with his fleet, heading somewhere else.

I grimace when that image hurts. I... I don't want to leave him. He has been trying to help me, even though our start was bumpy and chaotic.

He holds me tighter and pulls the blanket up to cover us. He is warm and I don't mind staying with him for longer. For longer than a day.

Chapter 35

Vrek

I hold Serena's soft body to me. Heat is still echoing through me and it gets stronger and stronger along my markings. My heart is still racing even though I stopped fucking her a minute ago. She strokes the scar from the beast's attack with a scowl. There seem to be tears in her eyes, which I don't understand.

Does she not want to go home?

I only brought her back on the spaceship because that forest wasn't a good place for her. But when she holds me like this, it's hard to refuse. I didn't plan to fuck her either, but... I guess I should have known when I came here.

Her sweet scent is so tempting for me to keep her forever.

Maybe I'm more than certain that I want her to be here with me. She doesn't seem to hate that thought as much as she once did once she started interacting with the other uzains.

Thinking about that sends a fire burning in me. She should be mine, not any other uzain's. I don't care what they think about her. I'm going to...

Well...

My chest aches. Everything about my plan for tomorrow feels wrong.

Who am I fooling? I want her more than I can admit to myself.

What Captain said earlier comes into my mind again. Maybe I should give it a go.

Last time, she moved on from the question without actually giving me an answer. How bad will it be if I ask again?

She can say no and that's going to be all about it. I can make the ask. I'm the male here and I think she likes me.

"Serena."

"Yea?" She blinks, seemingly trying to hold back tears.

I grit my teeth, trying to not give the tears too much thought. "You see, we are here now."

"And?"

"Maybe..." Fuck... Why can't I just say it out loud? "Like... more doughnuts?"

What the fuck am I saying?

"Oh, I suppose I can make some before the spaceship lands tomorrow." She sounds upset... Maybe it is dumb for me to ask for more. I didn't even mean to ask about that.

"No, I mean... More doughnuts beyond tomorrow."

Fuck... How much dumber can I be? My tongue is failing me!

She blinks and watches me without saying a word. Now, I'm supposed to follow up and actually ask what

I meant to ask. I sit up. Maybe the soft and comfortable bed is making it too hard to focus. I can do that. I'm a pretty good uzain and I'm good enough to be her mate.

"Serena, I've been wanting to ask." Fuck, is this even going to work? "Will you be my mate? Stay here with me? Like, spend time here with me and... I'll protect you, so no one will ever hurt you."

She also sits up. "Are you sure about that?"

"Yes. Captain will be the only tough one to fight against, but if I give that my all, I'll win. My horns aren't that bad."

She holds my arm and strokes me. My heart races in me and I resist the urge to keep talking. What else does she need before she will agree? We know we are perfect for each other.

She says, "So, you are going to keep me around so I will have to keep making you doughnuts."

"No, yes. I mean, I won't say never make any, but I want you as my mate, that's the most important thing."

She watches me with those tempting eyes and tasty lips that lure me to her. "I... I don't know."

"What do you need to be sure?" My markings are burning again. I need this to work. Why doesn't she like me?

She reaches her hand to my head. I lower my horns to her. She strokes my horn. "Look, I'm grateful how you kept saving me."

This doesn't sound good. What if... Maybe...

She continues. "Don't you think... I don't know... I'm not a uzain and I don't think Captain—"

I growl and interrupt her. "I don't care what Captain or any other uzain thinks. I only care about what you think. I'm certain I want you as my mate."

She blinks with a smirk. "Does that mean I will get to do whatever I want?"

What does that mean?"

She keeps going. "And you will bring me food whenever I want?"

Wait... Is that what human mates do? I've met humans before, but I've never looked into how human mates work. Is there something I should be mindful of?

"Yes, I'll bring you food and everything you want."

"Everything?"

"Well, what do you want?" Now... she is making me nervous. Is there something dangerous for the male mate to a human female?

She bites my shoulder. Her teeth don't hurt a lot, but... Fuck... The mild pain sends my cock twitching. If it is custom for the human female to eat the male, that won't be very fun. But for her... It will be worth it.

She watches me with a smirk. Maybe she is messing with me again. I haven't poked at that, but the doughnut magic? That has to be fake. She made it up so we will leave her alone. I think everyone else is just playing along to keep her happy.

Now, she has to be making up this biting thing.

She says, "If you want me as your mate, you'll have to respect me, which you seem to have a hard time doing."

"Well, I need to be tough and rough to protect you."

"Maybe I will need someone to protect me from you when you get naughty."

I grunt as my heart skips a beat. I can only hope she doesn't mean it. "Look, no one can protect you from me." I kiss her. "Be mine. I'll be the best mate you can ever imagine. And you know we are meant to be together."

I take her hand and put it on the marking on my chest. "Look, can you feel it?"

She is close, and my markings are burning hot. She should be able to feel that, right? She has no markings, so maybe she feels it differently.

She is such a tiny being who has my heart in her hand. I'm not a big fan of that, but watching her perfectly cute face, I can't hate her.

She runs her finger along my marking. "This is hot."
"Yes, for you."
"Oh..."

It feels like I'm on fire and I need her. If she says no... Do I keep asking? Do I insist?

She seems to give that serious thought. The smirk is gone from her face, replaced by a light frown.

She asks, "So, is it fine for you to have a mate who's not a uzain? Or are you messing with me?"

There is pain in her eyes. I hold her shoulders. "Look, I'll never lie to you, not about that. I'm not going to mess with you like that. I mean it: I want you as my mate. I know we didn't meet each other like most beings do, but I hope you will give me a chance."

She remains quiet and watches me. My heart races so hard that even when I was in the forest fighting the beast, it wasn't this bad.

I used to take what I wanted and pretty much do whatever as long as I followed the rules of the spaceship.

But... now I have to make this tiny human like me. I've tried...

She leans onto me. "Vrek... I... Yes, let's try this together. I still can't imagine being your mate, but at the same time, maybe it won't be that bad."

How dare she say something like that? She knows I'm a good mate. My cock twitches. I want her again already.

"Look, this is going to be amazing. Now, no leaving you on the space station."

"And you get to keep your allowance."

I grunt, but I won't think money is what she wants. Maybe that's it for us: we'll keep messing with each other until the end of the day, but she is going to be making doughnuts, so I'll always win.

"I have no problem letting you spend it. You can get food, toys, get whatever."

"Toys? Do you think I'm a kid or something?"

"Well..." I scratch my head. "Like, something fun?"

Her eyes narrow on me. "Look, maybe you should be smart about that now. I'm your mate, so you will have to be nice to me now."

Ah, that's what she wants, huh?

I grab her shoulders and push her onto the bed. "I'll be nice to you, and you will love this."

Before she can scream, I lick her pussy. She moans. "Fuck! You are crazy!"

"Oh, you bet."

She tastes so good, so sweet. Maybe I should have done this a long time ago. She moans and squirms, but it doesn't take long before she grabs the back of my head and shoves me against her pussy.

"Your tongue is so annoying!" She gasps and her pussy makes naughty and dirty noises.

"You taste amazing. My snack, and mine only."

"Fuck!" She screams and she squirts. I lick every drop of her sweet juice. "Vrek... You drive me crazy."

"You already agreed to be my mate. It's too late to regret it."

Will she though? I hope not.

She laughs. "Soon, it will be your turn to regret that. But you're lucky I kind of like you."

I grunt. "Kind of? You can keep lying to yourself."

She nudges my head. "Shut up and keep licking me."

"Everything for my mate."

I like this. It looks like she is happy, and that's all I need.

Chapter 36

Vrek

I go down the corridor as Serena is making doughnuts in the kitchen. It is my turn to count up everything in the storage room with the team so we know what to order on the space station. This is my favorite shift. There's no training where I sweat like a drenched animal, and there's no staring at the dashboard when the auto-driving system is golden and has never caused us any issues.

This shift is the only one when I can do something not taxing, but interesting.

The storage room is huge, but there aren't a lot of crates left since we have been flying for quite some time. I check the list while comparing it to stock in the area I'm assigned.

I think I have all the dried meat and seasonings counted and recorded.

Zil is a distance away from me. He is working on flour and grains. I hope he knows what he is doing. If we run out of doughnuts, that's not good.

I head over to him when I get my portion of work completed. I can't help the smile on my face and I decide to stop fighting it.

There is a hum in my chest and everything seems to be perfect. The day could only be better if I was with Serena. After my shift is over, I'll be staying with her and no one gets to separate us anymore.

Zil lowers the tablet and nods. "Hey, what's up?" He sniffs at me. "Hm... You are so happy today. It seems like you're bouncing. What's with the serious warrior?"

I clear my throat. "Look, I'm very serious and very professional with my work. I don't even know what you are talking about."

He shrugs with a smirk. "Well, who are you lying to? It seems like you are going to have a talk with Captain soon after this."

I sigh. "Do you think that's what's going to happen?"

Zil looks at the others, who are also working and don't care about us. "You have to anyway. He is going to find out soon after. But, she agreed, right?"

My cheek burns. "Yeah... I know I'm not supposed to, but..."

Zil eyes me up and down. He doesn't seem to be surprised at all. "I don't think Captain is that dumb. Everyone knows you are crazy over her."

My cheeks burn at that. "What do you mean?"

"I know from the way you look at her. More importantly, when you fought Captain and ran over to save her, we all knew. Just tell Captain before he comes asking. Better to admit it beforehand."

"I mean... I know he knows, but he won't be happy about this. Don't get me wrong. She is my mate now and nothing can change that. Yet..."

"Do you still want to stay on the ship?"

"I do. Do you think it is possible?"

The ring of the bell cuts us off. It is the end of this shift and we are supposed to submit our work and move on to the next thing. My next slot is empty, which is usually time for lunch. But for today, it means the spaceship is getting ready to land.

The broadcast soon confirms that. The spaceship is landing in a short while. Everyone other than the driving crew will go to the treasury to get their allowance for this landing.

Zil's eyes brighten. "Look, you can stand here and keep pondering, but I'm heading out now."

I guess the smart way is to talk to Captain, so...

It takes a while, but I find Captain at the door of the kitchen. No one else is there waiting for the doughnuts. Either they are getting their allowance or they are scared of Captain.

He turns around when I'm a few steps away from me. "Vrek..."

"Captain, morning."

He checks his watch at once. "I suppose. What do you have to tell me while the doughnuts are getting ready?"

"Well, Serena is my mate now."

"Marking her for yourself?"

"She already agreed. She is my mate now and nothing can change that."

"Are you implying I may do something otherwise?"

I huff. "We know how good she is. But I'm not backing off."

He watches me with menacing eyes. Is he getting ready to fight me? My horns are ready for that. I'll win, even if it means I'll have it bad. He won't win easily either, if he even stands a chance.

He says, "Looks like you are dead set about her."

"I am."

"I could see that the moment you brought her onto the ship. You aren't that crazy just for doughnuts."

Huh? But he agreed as the captain. I wasn't the only one who wanted doughnuts. But I can't deny that she is the one who caught my eye like no other.

But if that's what the captain thinks, I'm not going to argue. It sounds like it will be to my advantage. "Maybe. She is perfect for me."

I clench a fist and flex my arm. I'm ready to fight if I need to.

Captain eyes me up and down as if he is looking for a chance. But he isn't going to find a gap.

He says, "Looks like you think that I'm going to fight you."

"Aren't you?"

"I don't mind if you get a mate."

Really? That's not what I imagined. "So, will she get to stay on the ship with me? Or... Do I get to stay on the ship?"

He folds his arms and shows off his horns. "The rule hasn't changed. As long as you follow the rules and stay focused on why you are here, I'll allow that. You understand why you are here and why she is here."

"She's my mate."

"I mean the reason why I even allowed her to be here."

I suppose that's what a battleship means. We, uzains, are here to fight and battle. If we are so badly injured that we can't keep going, we will be sent back to the base-camp. And it seems like if Serena can't or won't keep making doughnuts, she will be kicked off the spaceship. But I'm going to take this for now.

I nod. "I'll bear that in mind. I think she understands, too."

It's good when no fighting is needed.

Captain says, "I think everyone knows. The way you look at her gives everything away."

"You still tried to take her away from me."

"So she wouldn't keep distracting you and making you into a walking soulless being. But I guess she already took your soul."

Hmm... I don't know about that. But maybe Captain isn't wrong. It hadn't been long since she and I waved each other goodbye and got on with our day, but it feels like it has been ages and I need to be right next to her already.

"Hey! Only the two of you are here?" Serena looks out from the kitchen. The scent of freshly made doughnuts rushes out of the kitchen, nudging me to scoop them into my mouth.

Serena tiles her head to the side. "Well, the two of you have your eyes glowing. Are you that hungry?"

Captain takes a step. "Look, I can have doughnuts all the time."

I want to go inside the kitchen first, but it won't be worth it to go against Captain at this moment. He is going to want the first one, and I don't really care about that anyway.

He picks up a doughnut. These have pink frosting and they look amazing with a dash of white powdered sugar on top of them. He starts eating with a smile. I reach for one when he hisses at me.

Serena rolls his eyes. "Come on. Both of you are big uzains, but you are here fighting over doughnuts. Everyone can have some, okay?" She takes one from the tray and hands it to me.

I take a bite before anyone can take it away from me. The inside of it is so soft while the surface is crispy. With the icing and everything, this is a perfect doughnut. Serena keeps making these perfect ones and it's getting hard to stop myself.

I take another when Captain is too busy with the two in his hands that he isn't quick enough to stop me.

This is so good.

She watches us with a grin. She might be laughing at us for hurrying for doughnuts, but at least she's happy.

I'm about to say something when the broadcast sounds. The spaceship is landing in a minute and we should get ready.

Captain groans. "I'll be back and there shall be doughnuts."

Serena shrugs. "But fresh ones will be nicer. Also, what if you find something on the space station to try out?"

He rubs his horns and I want to punch him in the face. He doesn't get to talk to Serena like that. He should use some more respect and—

"Vrek, you will come with me. Serena, you hold tight while we land."

Fuck... He just won't let me have a good time with Serena.

Captain starts walking with big strides. I let out a soft sigh and follow him. Serena smirks and winks. Now, I wish I knew how to make doughnuts, then I could probably stay here with Serena.

Before I leave the kitchen, she comes over and hugs me. I pat her back, but at the same time, I don't want to let Captain see this.

She pecks a kiss on my lips. "I'll miss you.."

A stream of heat rushes to my cheeks. "I love you."

"Good. You're the best."

I hug her back and squeeze her ass. "When he comes back for doughnuts, I'm going to come back to what's mine."

She chuckles. "Sure, I'll wait for you."

I stroke her back another time before I let her go. I have to before Captain will be mad at me again. "See you."

I turn to the door when her fucking hand... She strokes my cock and hurries her way to the other side of the kitchen and winks at me again.

Fine...

When Captain and I are out of the kitchen, he turns around to me. "Look, you are so crazy for her."

"I'm not ashamed of that. I'm glad she gives me a chance."

He muses. "You are different now."

Is that a good thing?

He looks to where we will be heading. "Keep up the good work. Otherwise, I'll have to take care of her for you."

Hell no. Serena is mine, and we like that.

Chapter 37

Serena

I peek out of the spaceship at the space station. It is almost time for the takeoff, but Vrek is still nowhere to be seen.

What happened? Is everything fine?

He told me to get on the spaceship first while he had to help the rest of the team to move stuff.

Those are there moving crates at the tail of the spaceship, but Vrek isn't there with them.

There aren't a lot of crates left by now, but Vrek is still not there.

Will they take off without him?

I shake my head. That probably won't happen as long as Vrek is with the Captain. Both of them aren't around and no one knows what happened to them.

No one knows what is happening, and the captain does what he wants. And since it isn't time yet, no one is looking for Vrek either.

Maybe I should have stayed with him. But Captain also told me to head back first.

"Serena."

"Zil. What's up?" I turn around, barely pulling my gaze away from the outside of the ship.

"Are you worried about Vrek?"

"Yes. I wonder where he is. I mean, he should be with Captain, so everything should be fine. But at the same time..."

"Well, who knows what's on Captain's mind?" He stares ahead too. "Maybe they are there to get in touch with someone who is paying us, or will pay us in the future."

"I still don't understand. Vrek told me someone hired the fleet to blow up that village, but he didn't know who that was."

"Yeah, I'm not surprised. The captain is the one who looks for those deals."

"So, the fleet is up for hire?"

"For whatever the captain is interested in."

"Are there other uzain ships out there?"

"There are. We have a basecamp somewhere for the young uzains and everyone who isn't on a spaceship."

"Oh... Are you the ones who swear to fight against the Empire?"

He clicks his tongue. "Yes and no? We don't like the Empire, but we aren't dead set on beating them. We are here for our own good. The planet where basecamp is can use our help. The best and fastest way to amass the wealth we need is to be off the planet and look for deals."

"It's like working and sending money home."

"Yes. And along the way, if there are things we can do that bring in more than money, that's even better. But if needs be... Well, I don't think Captain will steep lowly for money, but that's a possibility regardless."

"What's wrong with basecamp? Is it on a less developed planet?"

"Well, you will know when you get there. Vrek's time on this ship won't last forever."

"What? I don't understand." I would have grabbed his throat to ask more questions if that was easy to do so. But Zil is a bit too tall for that and I will only look dumb.

"Oh, it's not something bad. Every five years or so, we can opt to go back to basecamp and some retire. Though one can still join again."

"Do you think Vrek will get off the spaceship?"

He shrugs. "I don't know. Maybe? Eventually, every one of us has to. When you get old, you won't make for as good a warrior as we do now. Like, eventually."

Hm... That's interesting.

At the far end of the parking lot, there are two beings heading in our direction. Looks like both of them are in good shape.

Zil chuckles. "But maybe Captain will want to keep you on the ship, since you make the perfect food."

"I can also fix your bread."

"Huh?" He frowns and is seemingly clueless about how bad their bread is.

"You will understand when I make actual edible ones."

"I'll trust everything you make." He grins like a kid. Maybe every uzain is hungry for great food. Poor beings.

Vrek and Captain arrive. Vrek hurries to wrap his arms around me. "Aw, I missed you."

Captain huffs and groans. "Come on. It isn't that long since you were apart."

I hug Vrek back. I miss him too. "You're finally back." He is still the huge guy who gives me perfect warm hugs.

Captain rolls his eyes. "Zil, go help with the stock. Vrek, about what I just told you?"

Vrek nods. "Sure, I'll let her know about that."

Her? That's me, right?

We go back into the spaceship when Zil heads to the loading area.

Captain is gone soon enough, leaving Vrek and me in the corridor. I ask, "What was that about? What did the two of you talk about? If I can know."

"You can. He wants me to make everything clear to you. And the only important thing is that; he wants you to take shifts with the kitchen crew."

"So, I'll have to work now."

"Well, you want everyone to respect you, right? And, while we all love your doughnuts, you can be doing more."

"I understand. Like I told Zil, maybe I'll also fix your bread."

"Oh, the bread that you hate."

"I like bread and baked goods. But your bread is pathetic."

He groans. "I'll wait for what you got for me."

I stand on my tiptoes, but I'm still too far away from his lips. He leans over and kisses me. I stroke his back again. "But you spent so long with him; that can't be all you said."

"Well, that's nothing big. We met the one hiring us and collected payment, pretty much that."

"Oh, can I know who that is?"

He shrugs. "I would tell you if I knew."

"Huh?"

"The guy we met is a very forgettable one. There is no indication of who he works for. I mean, from what we attacked, you could guess. But nothing is solid. Who knows? The Empire has plenty of enemies."

"Has to be secretive, huh?"

"You bet. They have to. We know the state we are in. No one wants a war."

I nod. That's not wrong.

He hugs me again. "Don't worry about that. I miss you and we are finally together, that's what's important."

He kisses me and his hot lips light my body on fire. I love this. The markings on his body get hotter, as if he is burning, too. He holds me close to his chest, with his strong muscles wrapping around me. He is such a crazy uzain, but I like him this way.

I stand on my tiptoes, tasting his lips more. The broadcaster beeps and we jump, hurrying away from each other. My heart races so hard that it may jump out of my chest.

Even when most of uzain on the ship probably know Vrek is my mate, I still don't need to be spotted kissing him and hugging him in the corridor.

No one is around, so that's better for us.

Vrek sighs when the message is over. "Guess we should get ready for take off."

"Do you have a shift coming up?"

He shakes his head, but he seems upset about it.

I lift my brows at him. What's the problem? I thought no shift was better.

He says, "The broadcast ruined the mood."

"But you don't have a shift and I think we should be sitting or something when we take off." I glance at the corridor, making sure there's no one there before stroking his cock. "And, we aren't supposed to stay here in the corridor."

His eyes darken and he smirks. "Look at you, such a naughty one."

"What are you going to do about that?" The fire in me is burning again. He always does that to me.

He growls and picks me up into his arms. "You are going to regret being a tease and a brat."

"Make me." I can't stop a smile spreading on my face.

If this is how it will be for the coming days, I have nothing to complain about. "Vrek."

"What?"

"I think I like you."

He groans. "I love you, my mate."

I pat his chest right before he dashes into his room. Maybe I love him too.

Epilogue

Serena

I let out a breath and collapse on the chair. Finally, my shift in the kitchen is over. It isn't as bad as I thought and I've started to get used to the workload. The uzains treat me well too. They understand that I'm a small human and some of their tools and expectations make no sense to me.

"Hey, are you fine?" one of them asks with a frown.

"I'm good. I just don't want to sit down slowly like I probably should." I'm going to say something more when the timer on the oven beeps.

I get up when they hurry to stop me. "Here, we can take the bread out."

"Sure." I don't mind sitting back for them to do the job.

One of them takes the tray out of the oven and sets it on the kitchen island. "So, this is what you mentioned before. Your kind of bread."

"Yeah, give it a try."

I wanted to fix their bread, but I've been busy learning my job. This is the first time in a while for me to have the time and for the uzains to strangely not want doughnuts for snacks. And that may have to do with me telling them how I want to try out new recipes. Maybe they just want whatever I put out for them.

Watching their smiles may be my new favorite. It's not that bad compared to the cafe I used to own, which I don't think I'll be heading back to anytime soon.

Vrek is here with me, so there isn't a lot of reason for me to head back. I've talked to my helper there since and she is taking over the business, so that may be for the best.

The uzain chefs tear off pieces of the bread and eat it. They exchange a look with each other.

The head chef blinks. "This is so good."

The others nod and they try even more. I'm happy about that, like always.

There is a knock at the door. The head chef tells whoever it is to come in.

It is Vrek and he comes in to watch everyone else looking at each other. Vrek clears his throat. "Hello, guys. I wonder... Hm... Can I try that?" His eyes are on the bread already. "It smells so great."

"Sure." The head chef gestures at the bread and Vrek comes over with wide strides as if he worries that the bread will disappear before he gets there.

He takes a piece and his eyes light up. "Oh! This is so fluffy and soft."

I chuckle. "See? I told you I was going to fix the bread."

The rest of the chef team looks at each other with smiles on their faces. The head chef says, "Teach us your way tomorrow. Now that our shift is over, we are leaving. See you later, Serena."

Oh... Now everyone is leaving. They don't leave without taking some bread for themselves and almost empty the tray, but still. Now, there is only Vrek and I in the kitchen.

He eats some more bread. "I like this so much. It reminds me of... Well..." He frowns as he thinks while I can't stop smiling. Look at him, he has a pretty handsome face when he is in thought.

He finishes his bite and leans closer to me. "Look, it reminds me of your soft body."

I shiver from the spike of heat he sends into me. "Really? Are you going to eat me like you ate the bread?"

He growls, "You are such a tease." He grabs me and bends me over the kitchen island. "Another shift won't start any time soon. You're going to regret tempting me."

"Except maybe not, unless your cock is underwhelming."

"No fucking way!" He yanks off my trousers and my panties in one shift move. "You are soaking wet for me. Do you get wet just by looking at me?"

He lifts his brows and rubs my clit. "Or... Is it that... You were just so turned on by all the uzains around?"

What the fuck? "Geez, you are crazy. Come on... We know what you always do when our shifts are over and we get together."

"Ah, I like how you're expecting this."

"Yeah, but no— Oh! Fuck yeah!" I moan when he pushes his huge tip into me. I still don't understand how I can take his massive cock and enjoy him, but it is what it is. My toes curl. The bands on his cock rub against me as he goes deeper and deeper.

"What were you talking about? Keep going."

I moan as he hammers at my sensitive spot. "Fuck... What are you even doing? You can't even wait until we are in our room?"

I shiver as the cool surface of the kitchen island tickles my boobs. He goes harder and harder against me. My body is shaking, so much so that maybe the kitchen island is also shaking. "What if someone comes in?"

"They can watch how good you're taking me."

Fuck... My pussy squeezes at him even harder. I want this annoying cock and his annoying ass. Fuck it. He stretches me harder than I can imagine, and it's so amazing.

"Shut up! Your dirty mind is—"

"What you love. I know that." He picks up speed, sending waves and waves of pleasure through my body. I'm burning and, fuck, how can I love him even more?

"I hate you."

"Except you don't. You just hate to admit how much you love me." He squeezes my ass with his huge hand, slamming his cock even harder into me. He knows exactly how to destroy me with that cock.

"Fuck! Vrek! Yes!" I scream as an orgasm explodes in me. Maybe there are uzains walking by, but I can't control myself anymore.

He holds the back of my neck, gently pushing down as he leans over and presses his muscular chest onto me. He is so hot. I imagine his eyes glowing and dark at the same time. "Serena... I don't know why I keep wanting you. This is crazy. My perfect mate."

"Mmm... Love you."

"I love you too." He grunts and shoves his thick cock into the deepest part of me and his cock twitches, pulsing in his hot cum. "So tight. And squeezing me so well."

I want to wrap my arms around him, but the way he rides me from behind with that huge body slamming into me is more than I can take. This is the first time we've done this in the kitchen. With how horny he gets, maybe he is going to get us to do something else that's as crazy soon.

He kisses my neck. "I love you." He flips me over and takes my lips. I kiss him back. My body is melting in his arms.

I pat his back. "You are such a huge guy."

"Is that a good thing, other than how I can give you my big cock?"

I chuckle at that. "That's all you can think about."

He licks his lips. "Yes, when it comes to you, it's hard to think about anything else."

I knew it. He is just the way he is. "You've probably been thinking about that since we met. You stole me from the cafe."

He rubs his horns. "Well, I started out wanting doughnuts, but maybe I had already taken in your sweet scent and couldn't stop wanting you."

"You sensed your mate."

He tickles my chin. "Probably. You have no idea. My markings are burning for you."

"Does it hurt?"

He groans and his cock twitches. "The markings don't, but..."

"Are you so hard that it hurts? Right after you came inside me?"

"I can never have enough of you." He spreads my legs again, his cock already aiming at my entrance. "Sit up and take my cock."

"Again? You are crazy! This is the kitchen."

"Where food and snacks are prepared and consumed, yes." He pushes into me again. I arch and move, making it easy to take him in.

Maybe he isn't the only one getting horny all the time.

I reach my arms to him and he holds me. I may choke, like always, but when he wraps me up like that, he seems to be even larger and stronger.

His cock twitches and gets larger again. "Admit it, you like how I devour you."

"Mm... You better actually devour me like you said you would."

"Deal."

I love that handsome face.

I don't think we're supposed to be fucking around like this. Captain is going to be so mad if he finds out.

But to hell with that. I'm here with Vrek and that's the most important thing.

A big horny guy, just for me.

Get a bonus story!

https://icepawpress.com/alina-riley

He doesn't even know what's an Easter Bunny but he hates my event before I can even host it...

This grumpy and annoying gray alien with a tail hates me the moment I show up at the doorstep of the community center. For him, any celebration is stupid. Except I'm going to host the party for the kids and I'm going to do it amazingly well. He won't get to stand in my way. Everything is going great until... my partner for the event falls sick... Now, I need someone to help me with the bunny costume...

Also By Alina Riley

A Mate For The Luraella Traders
Saved by The Alien Boss
Guarded by The Alien Boss
Rescued by The Alien Boss
The Alien Boss's Hook Up
Crashing into an Alien Tribe
Trapped by Snow
Caught by Fire
Stranded by Vine
Mated to the Baekex Bandit
Taken by The Alien Bandit
Saved by the Alien Bandit
Healing the Alien Bandit
Mated to the Zalcor Rebels
The Space Outlaw's Treasure

Also From Ice Paw Press

Dark and Steamy Paranormal Romance
The Wolf's Captive: Collateral

Urban Fantasy
The Hidden Order of Magic: Shaken
The Magic Rebel

Steamy Sci-Fi Romance
A Mate For The Luraella Traders
Crashing into an Alien Tribe
Mated to the Baekex Bandit

Dark Mafia Romance
Kneel to the Jarockis